ACQUAINTED

WITH SQUALOR

Short Stories

By NATH JONES

Edited by SALLY ARTESEROS

LIFE LIST PRESS

CHICAGO · 2015

Life List Press
Chicago, IL

Copyright © Nath Jones, 2015
All rights reserved

PUBLISHER'S NOTE

These selections are works of fiction. Names, characters,
places, and incidents are either the product of the author's
imagination or are used fictionally and any resemblance to
actual persons, living or dead, business establishments,
events, or locales is entirely coincidental

ISBN-10: 1937316157
ISBN-13: 978-1-937316-15-0

Previous publications: "Norma L." From the Edge of the
Prairie 4 (2007): 69-76. Print.

Book design by Gin Y. Havard
Author photo by Louisa Podlich
Cover image by Yulia Drozdova

Printed in the United States of America

For Darek

ACKNOWLEDGMENTS

John Groppe, Bob Garrity, Sally Arteseros: the collection's literary editor, Lucille Fridley: copy editor, Gin Y. Havard: digital conversion specialist and technical implementation consultant, David McNamara: print layout, Chris Foresman: cover design, Mike Novak: sound engineering, Ryan McDaniels: audiobook narration, Toby Holsman, David Sincox, Bob Callahan, JT Lundy, Deva North, Yasin Patel, Gale Erie, Ryan Connor, Tom Kress, Alan A. Larson, Zach Dodson, Ryan Bradley, Nate Dean, Matt Hlinak, Meg Knodl, Matt Wood, Melody Layne, Nick Martin, Nathan Rule, Cindy Martin, Joyce Rule, Gary Rule, Lisa Suhr Fenner, Paul Mason, Jeff Rayburn, Susie Rayburn, Rachel Rayburn, Adam C. Lack, Rose Fauster, Matthew Havard, Evan Havard, Reg Gibbons, Sandi Wisenburg, Barbara Croft, Patrick Somerville, Everyone at Northwestern, Mama Moonrose, Xavier Rodriguez, Tom Arnold, Tom Martin, Josh Karaczewski, The Egans, The Chesaks, The Moreths, The Wells Girls,

Princess Buttercup Burkholder, Larisa Parrish, Tammy Servies, Damaris Melendez, Ecola Jackson, Hugh McGuire, Jane Friedman, Darren Mast, Andrew Groh, Alex Philbrick, Rob Sowder, Chad Anderson, Mark Rayburn, Amanda Douglas, Morgan Kiger, MJ Sorvillo, Skip Sorvillo, Mira Zakosek, Kruno Zakosek, Davorka Zakosek, Alejandro Bonilla, Nuri, Everyone at Standard Parking, Beth Wilson at Friar Tucks, Larry Hienrich and Tom Zanarini of The Dram Shop, Gus Mavraganes and Luis Acosta at Stella's Diner Chicago, Sam Veilleux, Jennifer Wohlberg, Isaac, Genevieve Jones, Ilze, Lori, Stephanie, Joy, Lisa Glancy, Michael White, Micah Ross, Chris Howard, Dariusz Janecki, Ardith Thompson, Pat Bruce, Maria Kubiak, Timothy Garrison, Truda Stockenstrom, Jenny Johnson, Amy Wheeler, Becky Holzman, Brenda Mangels, Scott Fridley, Austin Fridley, Daryl Fridley, Amy Vidovic, Christian Xavier, The Baristas at Intelligentsia on Broadway, Scott W. Smith, Steph Curtis, Jim, Dave & Noel Gale, Erin Gunderson, TJ Pinelli, Harriet Jonquiere, & Dorothy Jones

"Make it extremely squalid and moving," she suggested.

— J.D. Salinger

TABLE OF CONTENTS

DUST IN THE CLOUD

Eight-year-old Brian stood cavalierly on the top railing of the bridge, laughing at my faith in him. It was August 13th, 2009, the day before my family moved away. I was six, nearly seven. Brian and I were about to jump in the river but I was hesitant.

The city guys had just finished replacing the old rusted iron bridge that barely held a road together. New concrete reflected so much August sunlight. I stood in the sunshine and squinted, looking up. Brian did this boy thing, the first time that sweet way: moved his body to block the sunlight for me, helpful almost. In his shadow, I could open my eyes fully, really see him. But the instant I trusted him, really relaxed, he refused to be trusted, and jerked his whole body sideways—so fast I got almost blind, staring straight into the sun. It was a game for him. As soon as I shielded my eyes, he came right back and blocked all that light again, as if of course I could rely on him.

My arm drifted down to my side. I tried to accept his protective gesture but felt unsure when I looked up at his proud-of-himself grin.

There was this moment that almost seemed to matter, as much to him as to me. I could maybe have said something then, told him my family was moving away. But he seemed to get nervous about me gathering the courage and shifted his body again, laughed loudly and blinded me. That time my arm snapped up, ready for the betrayal.

Love is different from how I felt about Brian. Love makes everything okay, lets what's important last. That's not how it was with him. But we were always together.

I was about to protest, just leave him balanced there on that guardrail and go home, but he bent down slightly, extended his hand, and splayed five tan fingers toward me. "Come on, Dana! Get up here."

At home in the basement I knew my dad must have been twisting the knobs on his ham radio. All day he would be down there like that, sipping a two-liter of flat orange pop that'd get all warm, using Q-codes to listen to the ionized trails of meteors. You can hear them during the day. During meteor showers Daddy would sit there forever clutching the pop lid, turning it over and over in his hand, real slowly, listening. He endured so much static for that *ping!*

Not the night before, but the night before that there'd been a fight. A great big Mommy and Daddy fight where the walls shook because one of them wouldn't pretend to be less upset than the other. It got worse and worse until it became one of those awful screaming forevers. About facing reality, about almost the new school year, about no one thrilled about moving but what else? Mommy usually never yells like that; Daddy neither. But Mommy said her stuff over and over and Daddy came right back at her about why had she even told her mother anything, about not trusting him, about never being able to sell our house so why bother, about how ridiculous it would be to pay rent while losing money on a mortgage. He even asked her about Brian. She just screamed something back about why Brian would have any bearing.

I guess he didn't.

Maybe that's why I never told him we were going to move.

But I should have. Right then on the bridge before he laughed so hard, or at least some time that day. We were together the whole afternoon.

The fight between my parents had been over, but there was still this silence into our last day, the day of the most meteors since 1972. I was glad to be out of the house, away from the pressure. Shy, I guess, I stared at Brian's knobby body, at all those loose boy limbs and at his grown-out mess of sweaty curls jammed down under his hat. The sky went up, and up, and up so sunlit. Meteors came down invisibly. And he just stood there atop the guardrail, bouncing with that one hand's grabby insistence, with his head bobbing around, taunting me. I didn't say it, couldn't. I wanted a regular day, not some special good-bye. Beyond him, the river sloshed silently over silt-covered roots of leaning trees. Sulfurous water from the quarry rushed through the slimy culvert and fell splash-heavy into the endless brown silence of our slowpoke river.

That was our river—me and Brian's. It moved through corn and soybean fields, along property lines, past horse farms and that electric substation, the one my dad told us about with its circuit switcher, regulators, reclosers, and control building.

Part of the silence at home was Mom still mad, but part was real reverence for Daddy listening to the meteors. Even before the Perseids Dad was down in the basement a lot that summer. Not depressed, just listening to as much of the sky as possible. He'd already looked for a job. There weren't any. A lot of the time I would be down there with him, sitting on his lap. He called me Bony Butt and didn't want me to shift around because it'd hurt his thighs. So I'd stay still and listen. I'm like Daddy. I love all those sky pebbles out in the infinite void. Those rocks don't have to be attached to hope, but are. Only a fraction of them come close enough to us to burn up in a flaming rush.

Mommy tried to be nice. She would even talk about the comet's inbound orbit. Remind us that it was the sun, really, with its gravity, pulling Earth, pulling the comet, pulling all those fragments. But mostly she hurried by packing detergent, fabric softener, and Daddy's orange soap with the little bits of lava in it. You could tell she thought he should be reattaching the drain spout.

On the bridge Brian pretended to topple over to get my attention. I can't really be hurried, though. Mommy can. But not me, not Daddy. In the roadbed there were all these lines, more than the new bridge seemed to need to breathe. I looked down at that grated concrete, scratched my toe against it. I stood there undecided with my skinny legs, a yellow eyelet halter top, and two sun-bleached braids.

I don't know why this memory from three years ago has come back so vividly right now. We're having a lockdown drill at school. I'm under my desk, trying to pull my legs in so they won't stick out. But if I curl up, then my feet fall asleep. I hate these drills. I get all sweaty without being hot. Mrs. Nogarra just dead-bolted our classroom door. She pulled the blinds down in the windows, turned out the lights.

Out in the hallway I can hear the security dogs barking. Their claws click along on the floors, too. I'm not really scared. This is just a drill. When the K9 officers came two months ago, I got to walk the Belgian Malinois. Even if I'm not in real danger I still feel bad about not telling Brian we were moving. There's something about practicing for a day when you might die.

So Brian was on the guardrail, I was on the bridge looking up at him being so irritating and right then, I knew it was our last day together but Brian didn't know. I could have told him even though he was bobbing around like that between me and the sun. I do miss Brian. I was just mad. It seemed like he didn't deserve to know anything about my daddy's new job, the electrician-benefits-too job that Nana on my mommy's side had found. She set it up in May. Found a house near hers, too, kept saying we'd love the arched doorways. Daddy stalled, didn't want to go. At Nana's church there is this part of the service where you turn to the person next to you and say, "Peace be with you." And then that person takes your hand and says, "And also with you." I don't know if it has to be that way, but all the people in Nana's whole church say it every time.

Anyway so that last day with Brian, I could feel how really mad Mommy was, and sad. It had already been three months of waiting. During that big fight she said Daddy had to deal with what was coming, to accept it. He told her, "Not til after the Perseids."

Meteors flash through the sky but they don't disappear completely. There's this dust that remains in polar clouds, a tiny bit of something left lingering. So Brian and I were on the bridge about to jump and I stood there thinking about Daddy in the basement, about Mommy being mad, about metallic dust seeding clouds. It's the two ways, the Perseids. It's how the meteorite is disappearing—that truth of it burning up—but also the truth of how much remains after we've attached such joy to the momentary brightness. We don't really like that leftover stuff messing up clouds. The reality is, a rock enters the atmosphere. So what? That's nothing, kind of sad really. But if you're out there looking for meteors? If you drive into the country to see them tumble out of Perseus? Or if you're lying on your back on a sand dune, looking up? Waiting, hoping, watching so hard, totally mesmerized by the darkness and light? What's better? You're completely attuned and readied, in a way so different than when you're worried you'll get shot.

And then, especially if you're there together with

your favorite people, and someone sees one. There! It was right there! Isn't that everything worth waiting and hoping for? Brian didn't like it when I got lost thinking about my own stuff. He wanted me paying attention to him, expected me to watch everything he did. He didn't care that I got mostly bored with him being so dumb.

A quarry dump truck rumbled by. We waved to the driver. He didn't honk his horn, though, for whatever reason. The river just kept coming out from under the new bridge.

Brian's sneakers squeaked on the guardrail. He never stopped, never gave up. I tuned him out when I could, but his mock-jumping yanked me forward in time. The guardrail shook, rang resonant like a singing bowl.

I hate this. Right now, Mrs. Nogarra is following the lockdown protocol. She's sent a text to the principal's secretary saying we're all accounted for and that there's one extra kid in our classroom, Anna Hitchens, who was on her way to see the nurse for an allergy shot.

It's like I get stuck in all this confused frustration without knowing why. Anyway, so I was on the bridge, half-blind from the sun, listening to the guardrail, and Brian was bouncing up and down, reaching for me. He was done shifting around. He just wanted me up there by him. His five tan splayed fingers hurried me on.

There was this flapping hand thrust in my direction. What other devotion did I know? I took it from the blinding sky.

He yanked me up. I stood next to him, shut my eyes, and squeezed his hand. I rose up, stood on tiptoes. We were right there together. Not forever. For like two seconds, maybe one.

He didn't pull me, didn't count to three. He just jumped, and because I was holding on, both our bodies fell away from the bridge.

Down fast, then splash; my elbow touched the bottom. The water eddied around jagged limestone. I leaned back, and the panic of not wanting to jump seeped out of me. We were still holding hands. Letting go felt almost wrong but holding on in the current was hard. Our hands broke apart with a slight abruptness. He didn't seem to notice. I pretended the same inattention but can still feel how tight his grip on me was and his sweaty clenched assurance.

Brian swam faster than I wanted to go and stood up sometimes to check how deep the water was. He always wanted a sandbar. Then if he were standing on one, he'd demand enough water to dive and disappear into.

As we passed under a low branch, Brian grabbed it with both hands, lifted himself into a chin-up, then dropped down making a huge splash all over me.

"Brian!"

He stood up and spun around in a circle with his cupped hands moving fast on the surface of the river. The spray went everywhere.

"I hate you, Brian."

"So?" He made it sound like he didn't care. But I knew he did. "Don't put your feet down, Dana. You don't got shoes on."

Without agreeing to anything for real, I was floating downstream. "I'd have got shoes if you'd have told me we were going in the river. I thought all you wanted was to check out that rabbit's foot from the mailbox."

That's probably what Mom meant about him. You'd think you were doing one thing, think stuff was fine, and then all of a sudden he'd have you jumping in the river. I never agreed to that. We were just going to see what the mailman did with my rabbit's foot.

We had put the flag up on Mr. Schumacher's mailbox and hoped the mailman might take the furry blue bone to some other mailbox far away. Like maybe to Brian's step-sister's apartment, so she could have good luck with her OSHA fall protection training certificate. Brian ran towards Mr. Schumacher's mailbox after he came to get me and Mom finally let us go. I walked down the sidewalk yanking at the parts of my hair that Mom had pulled too tightly into the braids, loosening the constraints, relieving the pain.

That rabbit's foot was great. It was capped with brass and had a beaded key chain, the kind that snaps together if you have the patience to get the little skinny part of the chain through that little skinny part of the clasp where the tiny brass ball holds it in place. I'll bet Brian's step-sister would have really liked it.

By the time I caught up to him at the mailbox, Brian had already discovered that the mailman had left the rabbit's foot right where we'd put it. "Damn." He snatched the thing out of the mailbox so fast, took two propulsive steps, and threw my rabbit's foot as high as it would go up into Mr. Schumacher's old blue spruce.

So really, I'm not as guilty about not telling him we were moving away, because that moment made me so mad.

I hope this drill is over soon though. I'd stretch out and lie down on my belly but then Mrs. Nogarra would yell at me, tell me I'm not taking the threat seriously. Who cares? Why should I take a made-up threat seriously anyway? The police dogs aren't even barking close by anymore. I can hear them all the way over on the other side of the school doing their sweep by the music room.

That police officer who came to our school with the K9 unit was talking about protecting, serving, something. And then Mrs. Nogarra told us what domestic tranquility means, how important it is. Sometimes I'm not convinced that teachers know as much as they're supposed to. We did two worksheets on the Perseids. She didn't get everything right about Swift-Tuttle. Daddy says not to worry about it, says Mrs. Nogarra gets us from August to June, says we're mainly on our own.

Staring up at all those wiggling branches of the spruce tree by Mr. Schumacher's house I felt caught in the moment, almost trapped. Boys do that. I'd love to say they don't mean to, but they do. They like it when girls are almost about to cry but won't. And I wouldn't. But I wanted to go get my rabbit's foot out of the tree. I couldn't see where it went.

With that keychain part it could be hanging anywhere in that big tree. Probably still is. I gave up. "What do you want to do now?"

He had said, "Let's go down by the river."

"But I didn't wear any shoes."

"So." His tone was superior. "It's not like we'll go in."

I should have known we would, though. And there we were: in it. Brian scrambled up the riverbank and ran along these huge roots next to me. "Water moccasins love places like this," he said. I didn't show any fear. He picked up dried mud and leaves from jutting branches, ground them between his wet hands, whipped around again, and showered the filth onto my hair, my forehead. I shook it off as if it didn't matter. He cackled, so proud of himself.

The Perseids come at the earth so fast, thirty-eight miles per second. When you're watching the Perseids and helping to gather data as an amateur observer you're supposed to write down all the obstructions, all the reasons why you can't see every falling star. I suppose Mommy sort of had a right to be worried about Daddy. But whether she endured her fear or if it broke her, if she snapped and screamed that everything had to be a certain way, it didn't matter. The old job was gone and Daddy wasn't coming up from the basement.

Sometimes you have to really tell someone what matters most, so they know. I kind of told Brian my dad was in the basement but not really why. Not how Mommy walks by while Daddy tells her how many kilometers it is from the receiver to the transmitter and how that's his way of saying, "I'm sorry" and how Mommy knows it is, accepts it.

In the river, Brian was letting me, making me, watch him. He swam and threw branches as if they were spears and tried to run upstream. He bent down searching under the brown water for submerged rocks, pulling them up, hoisting them onto his shoulder first, and then shot-putting them over a particular branch, into a particular hole on the bank. He pulled my ankles and made me scream.

I floated and watched.

But I didn't want to have to. I said, "Why you gotta do that, Brian?"

"Do what?"

"Everything you do. All thrashing."

I hated Brian for not knowing how much it all matters. It was all too easy for him to destroy. But he didn't know it was our last day. I kind of thought Mom would have told his mom and then Brian would have known from that. But apparently not. Mommy said she didn't tell anyone and especially not Brian's mom because she didn't want to hear Brian's mom tell her to have a garage sale.

So no one knew. Mommy was packing boxes; she had the moving truck coming, but didn't feel like it was anyone else's business where we went and what we did.

But the loyalty, you know? I looked up into the summer swoosh of tossing trees. Air saturated with August heat surged over us and moved on, suddenly neglecting the banks lined with mulberry trees, with ash, cottonwood, and maple.

Regardless of what I said or didn't say, Brian ran up the bank and bolted down the grassy alley as I floated. He stopped to do something but I didn't look back because I didn't care. He was in such constant motion. Before I got adjusted to his rushing away, he was coming right back. I heard his sneakers scraping down the bank, gravel and twigs falling into the water. I flipped my hair back to get all the gross stuff off, dunked my head, and looked up at the sky. It was pale, sort of washed out and used up. The way it lacked magnificence irritated me. Brian came up behind me all commanding, "Shut your eyes."

"No." I didn't even think about whether I wanted to shut my eyes, I just said no because of the way he told me I had to. I was sick of doing everything I was told.

And then kinda nice but not really, he said, "Just shut your eyes."

So I did what I was told. I shut them. Because I guess he scared me some. I wanted to be good, too.

"Now, open your mouth."

"No way." I wouldn't do that. Not with my eyes closed.

"Just do it. I won't mess with you, I promise." He just wanted his way.

"Promise?"

Then, out of nowhere, he was really nice. Like he wasn't going to do anything mean or splashy. "I already promised," he said.

I was still leaning back in the water. I squinted, keeping my eyes mostly closed, and I could see the sweat over his lip, but still didn't quite trust him. He stomped around, shuffled his feet along the riverbed, kicking up too much silt on purpose, but the whole time he held something precious, so gently.

I didn't want to be afraid. Not when he was being for-real nice.

I hated the not knowing, floating with my eyes all the way closed again and not knowing why. It would have been worse to open my eyes and see him looking right at me.

So I shut my eyes, floated, opened my mouth.

I could feel that he was watching me. He started laughing. But I kept my eyes shut, kept my mouth open, and relaxed as much as I could.

He moved so close that I could feel the summer squeezed between us.

That water rippled everywhere the way it does when a quick gust touches down.

He was directly behind me then. I heard the current push around the sides of his waist. He pressed his belly against the top of my head, steadying both of us. I can still feel the waistband of those old green shorts. "Keep your mouth open."

I did as I was told, wanting him to be happy with me, wanting everything to be all right so that he would keep using that nice voice and not go back to the intimidating one.

The shadow of his arm caused the red behind my eyelids to darken. He dropped something right in my mouth but not all the way back. I realized it was a big, juicy mulberry as my tongue crushed the warm resistance.

"Good, huh?"

I nodded, and opened my eyes a little bit. He was smiling but the instant he saw that I saw him, he stopped. Pretended he hadn't been as happy as he was.

He moved carefully, being sure of his footing, and fed me berries, one by one, keeping some for himself, tossing his up into the air, tipping his head back to catch them, until he was finished sharing and threw the rest away against a flat cement fishing platform, without any thought at all. He was done. Didn't want to share anymore or be nice with mulberries.

I floated.

I shut my eyes again, enough so that he wouldn't yell at me.

Right then, in the river with Brian, my braids moved in the water—independently of each other, almost independent of me, like snakes, but nice ones, friendly. One crossed my neck, so slowly. I felt its soft woven weight against my throat. I can still feel that halter top tied across my back and neck.

"Dana! Check it out!"

Somehow without realizing it, I had passed him. He was twenty feet behind me. Brian was holding a turtle over the top of his head. I could see the box turtle's black legs, red-striped, clawing the air above our river. First the head disappeared. Then I saw those legs retract, and once the thing was fully in its shell, Brian heaved it right at me.

It's impossible to run away in a river. "Brian!" I screamed. But down it went, gone, probably landed on its back on the river bottom, upside down, legs flailing. It was down there forced to wait for whatever would flip it back.

I wanted that mercy to come from me. I groped along feeling for the turtle with my feet. It was gone. I moved my toes, squishing the silt, piling quiet mounds of warm mud on top of one foot with the other. The silt felt so good, heated by the summer sun beating down through the shallow river water.

"What are you doing?"

"I don't know. It feels good."

With three hard pulls he passed me, swimming all out.

I dove after him and we just floated together. Well not really together, but both in the river, kind of nearby each other.

He said—and I think this is the part that makes me feel bad—he said, "What do you want to do tomorrow?"

That was it. On the bridge it was kind of optional to tell him. But when he asked me straight out what we should do the next day? And I knew I'd be gone? That was the exact moment when I was supposed to tell Brian.

But I didn't. I ran two fingers down my braid in the water.

After a while, he gave up planning anything for the next day and said, "I wonder what time it is?"

"Why?"

"I'm supposed to be home when my mom gets home. I said I'd be there at four."

I was suddenly mad. "That was my rabbit's foot. You didn't have the right to throw it away like that."

He said nothing. That's how he was—no admission, no apologies. There was a breeze. The rippling water came closer until I felt the air moving on my wet neck and ears and let it go. "We're not gonna be back by four."

You can't be afraid of everything all the time, or mad.

Mrs. Nogarra's walking back and forth now, erasing stuff off the blackboard, getting ready to start class again whenever they say this drill is over. It's funny to think about someone really coming through the door, really shooting us all. There's a kid that sometimes walks too close to the lockers when everyone's in the hallways; maybe he would do something like that. But I don't think so, not really. He's just rubbing his shoulder along them, all weird. Even though it's nothing you can tell the teachers are watching him, and the principal is too. They do that with all of us. Like, once, there was this other kid who shouted something, I forget what, something stupid, some boy thing, and you would have thought he'd thrown a brick right through a window. One teacher grabbed him hard by the arm, another teacher grabbed him by the other arm and they were right down the hall to the psychologist.

I don't ever say anything.

But I'd never shoot a classroom of kids, either.

Who would?

That's the thing. They don't know and can't anticipate it. Because it's inconceivable, yet it happens.

Just not here. Hopefully not ever, not here, not at Brian's school, either.

I'll bet he has to do these same drills. But I know he's okay under his desk, hiding. Because I know he's probably playing that game where you shoot little wads of notebook paper through another kid's fingers held up like goalposts.

That's why I kind of really did love Brian. Because he helped me not take everything so seriously. Mommy and Daddy think everything should matter—all of it, the lid on the milk, everything. But then, if you're under your desk and your teacher's all worried about a pretend shooter, it gets a lot more scary than if you're just on the classroom floor with your friends, flicking paper.

All that day on the river I was thinking about how many meteors were raining down. Brian and I floated along. We couldn't see any of the Perseids but they were coming one after the next. I looked up, wished I could see just one meteor during the day. I stayed mad about him not telling me he was supposed to be home for his mom and said, scolding like, "You're gonna be in trouble, we both are. That's no fair."

"Why's it no fair?"

"I would have stayed with my dad, listening to meteors. Today might be a record."

"How's your dad going to know how many meteors fall today?"

"Meteorites, stupid."

You can really hear them, on that radio in the basement. There's this static, kind of a buzz, but then the pings are so clear, they ring out. Sometimes two meteors will come almost at once, but you can always hear the vibration of each, you know something's happening, you can feel it almost, right in your chest, the buzz between them, that disturbance, and then gone.

We floated but he moved away from me, ahead.

He always had to be ahead. Well fine. We were done with each other anyway, with the river, too, I could tell. No more keeping my head back wet and drifting, no more looking up into the unpredictable hot-summer rush-swoosh that tossed the green trees.

Brian and I didn't talk. He adjusted his hat. At the third bridge, we pulled ourselves out of the water and walked up the concrete slope. Brian ran up the embankment, stomping to make water squish out of his shoes. The white elastic of his waistband folded out from his tan back. Water made his green shorts hang funny, curved and low. He couldn't keep them up without wringing water out.

I made my way over the old rusted iron guardrail and caught up to him without seeming to try.

Cars passed us and the rushing summer wind felt good and started to dry us out. We walked back towards our street, not talking. Brian was being all Brian again. He waved to all the cars going by. Some drivers waved back. Some honked. One car, driven by a teenager, swerved toward us, and I grabbed Brian's arm.

"He ain't gonna really hit us, Dana. Relax."

People tell each other to worry about stuff and then say to relax.

I'd almost like to see some stupid kid with some stupid gun come into our classroom right now. Daddy told me what to do. He said to pick up a desk and throw it right at his face. I mean, right at him. I'll do it, too if it ever happens. Maybe I should tell Brian that I'm sorry for moving away without him knowing. Except, he was just so, I don't know, like a pouncer. We were walking along the road as a car slowed behind us. It was Brian's mom in a brown station wagon. He jumped up on the hood of the car and slid off, pretending she had hit him.

Brian's mom rolled down the passenger side window, the one by us, leaned over and said, "You two been playing in the river?"

Brian picked up a car antenna from the edge of the road. He poked at the front right tire with it. "Yeah."

"Have a good time?" Brian's mom was pretty. My mom wasn't, always covered in stuff from the garden, always in her old clothes.

Brian looked at his mom but didn't seem to notice anything like that. "We saw a turtle."

I felt Brian's mom looking at me in a way that I hadn't even noticed before. It was like she saw all of me at once, the outside and everything I was thinking, too. I didn't like it. I looked right at her, smiled, and then quit on purpose. She looked away, said something to her son that I couldn't hear.

I pushed my shoulders forward, suddenly aware of how my wet halter-top was clinging to me. I felt how small my shorts were. They were from last year. I must have grown a lot. I tugged at them and stayed quiet.

She shifted the car into park. "Want a ride home?" She leaned over and opened the front and back passenger doors.

Brian lunged onto the hot vinyl of the front seat and threw his wet hat on the dash. He started pushing the air-conditioning vents around so that the air would hit him. He kicked off his gross shoes, put his feet up out the window, real relaxed acting, then pulled his feet back in, put them down, and turned on the radio.

My feet felt raw against the hot asphalt. I had my hand on the door. I probably would have gotten in, but Brian snapped at me. "My God, Dana. Just get in the car."

That moment was exactly what I mean. He'd pounce all the time, never seem to listen, and then say stuff like that, so mean. Why? So, no. I don't need to go back and tell him I'm sorry. Because I'm not, really. As much as we were friends, we weren't.

I stepped back, didn't look at either of them— him or his mom. I stood there, maybe defending a tranquility of my own, thinking about meteors ping, ping, ping, ping, ping, ping, so many, thinking about Mom folding towels. And right then, I remember it now, I wanted to be away from him, just completely away.

I couldn't look him in the eye. I said, "I'm gonna walk."

Brian's mom looked worried, as though she cared. Maybe she did, or maybe she didn't like hearing about my mom's petunias all the time. I don't know. But she said,

"Honey, you don't have any shoes on. The sidewalk's not great. And there's a lot of glass."

I looked at the sidewalk. She was right. It was all broken, uneven, half weeds.

Brian looked at me, then at his mom, and said, "Leave her alone. It's not worth it. She's more stubborn than Dad." Then he looked back at me. "Why don't you just get in? We're going right where you need to go."

Yes, I was going home, which was still across the street from their house. But my home was about to change, the next day; the very next day I'd have a new home, the one I have now. It was like I had already started reorienting, though toward what I didn't know.

Brian got impatient, like always. "You're stupid. You could be home in two minutes. You were all worried about my mom not knowing where I was and now your mom's not gonna know where you are."

I shut their car door carefully. I didn't want to be anywhere in two minutes. I wanted something slower. I knew Mom wouldn't worry too much. Brian's mom would say I was coming. It wasn't just about getting home. It matters how you feel when you get there. I didn't want to jump in the car, feel bad about getting the backseat wet, be mad at Brian for rushing me and being mean, and then end up home two minutes later, still mad, flustered and telling Mom all the uncomfortable stuff, offering her nothing amazing about invisible meteors constantly lighting up without notice because of all the sunlight that can pierce so many treetops all at the same time.

Across the roof of the station wagon I saw an old black walnut tree standing in that riverside park, shading the road. There were all these walnuts that had fallen in the street and on the grass—everywhere—some green ones from that year and some black, split-open ones from the years before. None of the walnuts that fell on the road would ever be trees. It bothered me. I hated how many got run over by cars that didn't care. I didn't want to be in any car that would smash those walnuts and not ever let them be trees, but I couldn't say it. Brian would say it was stupid. And I couldn't say that their going where I was going didn't really matter.

Brian leaned back on the seat. I knew he was done. He'd only ever protest so much. Brian's mom leaned over and spoke directly to me through the window. "Dana, be sure you get right home and get a hot shower. That river is filthy."

I nodded. The car pulled away.

I was seething, not with rage, not with any baby, bratty tantrum, but something close to that, something nearly impossible to contain. I went back to the bridge, to the river, and stared out at how it kept disappearing forward. That motion, those calm interminable swirls, happen forever, whether you're there or not. But I was there.

I threw a handful of rocks over the railing and kept looking, trying to see it all, absorb everything about the place that was most my own, most ours. I didn't want to leave, I hated that I had to, hated all the ripples of every little rock. I hated being all wet with my braids still dripping down my hot back. I hated letting go when Brian's mom's car turned at the corner and disappeared.

I pretended like I hadn't seen it, and looked straight down at the river— those big, slow swirls untwisting out from under the bridge. I hated it, that constant motion.

Then I hated the stillness of it even more. Every rock-splash I'd made was gone. It looked like nothing had ever happened. But I couldn't throw more rocks, make more splashes that would just disappear. I wanted to be home hearing meteors moving through the sky, knowing they were happening. I only wanted part of everything, just the ice and ash ignited and falling, wanted every single one, all the Perseids. I wanted to get up to that dust in the cloud, to be with it, to make love last, wanted to be with Daddy in the basement, wearing his headphones, sipping flat orange pop during the whole thing, not crying, not mad, not sweating for no reason under a desk, not ever giving up all the big opening hopes attached to so many little pieces of the sky.

BLINDFOLDED ON SOME OLD
PEDESTAL

No one had made a summary judgment.

Chicago's new kind of February wrapped slick around the curb. Unknown to one another, two women waited in a glass shelter on Sheridan Road. Twenty-eight floors of brick and iron-trimmed windows stood behind them with an ash tree. Their bus must have broken down as it was already twelve minutes late. The older of the two women sat on a wooden bench looking north into the brake-slam traffic. She held her ankles together, her knees together. She sat up straight, rocked her feet back and forth, and kept both hands on her purse. Lady Justice had no place between them, really.

But the younger woman in a bright red skirt suit dragged all the shoulds and have-tos right into it saying, "Waiting for the 151?"

The older one nodded slightly.

The younger woman's mind reeled: *Don't look so put out, lady. It's just a question.* "I'm Marguerite. Do you live in this building?"

The older woman shook her head, did not elaborate.

Marguerite was already incensed. Maybe it had nothing to do with anything. Likely it was an overreaction to what wasn't even really a rude response. She'd demonstrate common courtesy though. "I do. That window right there, with the lined curtains. They're vintage. I got 'em on eBay. Look. See? Count up. Eighth floor. Ours is the one by the window with the sleeping cat. See it? That's where I live. With my kids. They can walk to school now. My ex hates it, says all kids should have a yard. But I don't even know what he's talking about. The park's right there—all that grass, bigger than anybody's yard anywhere they used to live. What's the big deal? My kids are old enough to cross a damn street before they toss a ball. Plus, walk under that overpass and there's the lake. How many kids have that?" Marguerite checked the time on her cell phone and pulled up a bus-tracking app. "It has nothing to do with having a yard. All it is is that he doesn't want to drive down here in Friday afternoon traffic. Those children might be old enough to cross a street but I'm not just putting them on the Blue Line. What if he's not there to pick them up? He did that shit to me. He's not doing it to my kids. No way." Marguerite looked at the woman to gauge her reaction. It was impossible to tell what she was thinking. She had on those big black sunglasses they give people after cataract surgery.

The woman behind the glasses did not respond.

Marguerite pressed her case. "He screwed my best friend's sister. I caught 'em. She tried to drive away. The whole neighborhood saw. Well. The stay-at-home moms. And my kids. They were in the back of my car. I probably would have gone all demolition derby on her if they weren't." Marguerite didn't bother looking for the bus. She knew exactly how long they'd have to wait. "My mother has a purse like that."

She made a moral point not to share any of the

route tracking information she'd just gleaned from her cell phone. The old lady would have to ask for it, would at least have to tell her her name. Then Marguerite would absolutely be nice in her response, be cordial, be polite— she would say how long it would be before the bus arrived. But until this old biddy said something, she wouldn't say a word, either. Marguerite tossed the phone deep into her big slouchy purse with as dramatic a gesture as possible and snapped at the woman, "What do you do?" It was like sniper fire from a rooftop, this question.

No response. A minute passed. The other woman rocked her feet forward and back likely to keep the circulation going, to keep them up off the frozen cement, and stared into the traffic looking for the bus.

Marguerite couldn't take this much unspoken tension. *That hair is unbelievable. It's so coarse. And those roots, that's like three inches of gray. Makes the dark brown look that much more washed out. How can some people just let themselves go?* She couldn't leave it alone. It was a passably appropriate question—to know the other's name, to ask what someone did. Why this perceptible wall of resistance? She put out a manicured hand and poked the woman's shoulder.

The woman on the bench pivoted, turning around fairly quickly. "Excuse me."

"I thought maybe you were deaf. Do you want my business card?"

"Somehow I've lived this long without it."

"What did you say? You're mumbling. Here. You're probably looking for someone like me."

"I doubt that I am."

"You have to speak up. I can't hear you."

"Would you listen if you could?"

"That I heard."

The older woman turned back, looking into the traffic for the bus like a pigeon that didn't want her feathers ruffled in the wind.

Marguerite used one acrylic fingernail to clean out the bottom of another. "You have daughters, don't you? You don't even need to answer that. I can tell."

Pedestrians crossed the broad street with the walk signal and dispersed. A homeless woman across the street picked through a trash can.

It became apparent that she wasn't going to get a rise out of this old lady. Marguerite tapped one nail against another. "Aren't you even going to look at that card?"

The woman with the roots took the card and held it out over her purse. She looked at the name, read aloud.

"Marguerite Zhenshky-Banks
Personal Images
Design   PR   Digital Couture"

She ran her finger over the raised ink twice, doubtless noticing how *Banks* was carefully crossed out with a permanent marker, and then politely put the card down on the bench next to her.

Marguerite tried not to notice. "I'll have new ones printed up when I have a proper office."

A taxi slowed to a momentary halt in front of them, put its hazards on, hopeful. Its driver beeped the horn twice, looked out the passenger window, then shook his head in disgust. The car sped away, weaving around bikes and other less savvy vehicles.

Marguerite said, "I hate when they do that."

The older woman nodded.

Marguerite was beyond annoyed watching the older woman's feet in perpetual motion. The silence of the action, of those orthopedic soles against the cement, was worse. She could not stand it—any of it—she wanted out. She should have gotten in the taxi, and she considered flagging down another. But she'd already waited this long. Worse, she didn't have the money for another overly-indulgent cab ride. She'd do anything to be rid of the moment, of the conversation, of the shelter, of the necessity of waiting for buses, of the inescapable nature of having quit smoking, of interminable conversations with co-workers about healthy food options, of tears that came at all the wrong times, of hidden motives and financial incentives, of teething children and uncontrollable men, of florists gouging people on major holidays, of dentists who add surcharges for the use of electronic apex locators during root canals, of useless insurance, of rented tablecloths, of cellphone apps that track locations to sell people's pathways, of that weird homeless person across the street fumbling around in trash cans block-by-block, of love that breaks down. Injustice lives in the unquiet heart. She accepted nothing, wanted none of it: not waiting for the bus, not having to be near this unresponsive woman, not this unending imperative to show up at her lawyer's office. It was the fifth time in three weeks. Marguerite refused it all. She grabbed an e-cigarette and snapped harshly, "God. What's wrong with you? Can you at least say something while we're stuck here."

"Well—"

"Well, nothing. Spit it out. What do you do?"

The old woman stopped rolling her feet. Both feet pointed straight up. Her knees touched, her ankle bones touched, her heels touched, even the edges of her shoes touched, but the toes touched nothing.

Marguerite didn't notice. If she had, she might have been aware of the tension in the woman's thighs, shins, and the tops of her feet: that restraint, that resistance. "Just tell me."

"I protect a man's dignity."

Nicotine vapor rose into the cold, gray morning. "That's intense. You're like part of an entourage? One of those old-time personal secretaries? Which man, is he famous, do I know him? How much is he worth? Do you have a good social media person? What's the URL for his blog? I'll put it in my RSS feed."

"I don't know what you're talking about."

"I'm talking about your job. This mystery guy. Whose dignity do you protect?" She shoved the e-cigarette back into her purse.

"My husband's."

"Oh."

The feet rolled down. Every tension was released. "Is that not good enough?"

"I didn't say that." That acrylic click. "But why would you do that?"

"What business is it of yours? It's what I do."

"I hear you. I get it. I'm dating a guy. Another one. He's okay, it's good. But I don't want to go through it all again, the phoenix rising from ashes bullshit. You know? If we're going to have little kids and play at the edge of the water together? Or. Whatever little happy memories we're going to have? I don't want that again and then have it smashed. If this guy's going to leave me after all that, like my ex did? After the Indian River citrus for everyone every Christmas? Then I don't even want any of the happy-happy, joy-joy bullshit. Because. You know why? I stood there in that courtroom. I was there. For what? It was a slaughter." Marguerite readjusted her waistband, hiked her hose, took her foot out of her shoe, moved the seam around her toes, jammed her foot back into the shoe, and hefted the big, slouchy purse up on her shoulder again. "Aren't you going to ask what I do?"

"You already gave me your card." The older

woman tapped the business card on the bench with an irritating fingernail of her own.

Marguerite wished the older woman would put the card in her wallet. "But I can elaborate. That's how this works. I read a guide about it, networking. I give you my card, then you're supposed to ask questions. That's how we establish a rapport."

"I don't think we're going to have a rapport."

"Why not? Because you think I should stay home and do some fool's laundry? Let that wench with the Mazda do his laundry."

"I didn't say you should do laundry."

"Who has time for it? Work. Commuting. Business trips. Custody hearings. Laundry is the last thing I have time for."

The woman in the cataract sunglasses looked up at the top of the bus shelter, as though wishing the birds had a place to land. Wire Vs poked up in a dense row, preventing the crossbar from becoming a comfortable perch for the birds. "Have you considered getting some kind of help? To relieve the tensions?"

Marguerite bristled at her own undoing, forgot about the business card, and sat down next to the older woman. "I've been seeing a therapist. She's useless." Stuffing her irascible mood back down into the presentable part of herself she said, "So where're you going today?"

"Downtown."

"Why don't you just tell me anything outright? Where downtown?"

"To a salon at Adams and Wabash. I need to get my roots done. They're starting to show. I never let it go this long. My husband has been home recuperating from—well, anyway. My hair's gotten just awful."

"Not it hasn't. I didn't notice at all."

"You're lying. You've been staring at my head this entire time. It's terribly rude."

Marguerite felt another incendiary urge. After just having gotten her respectable self back under control she wanted to push this woman right off the bench. But she did not. Instead she leaped away from the woman, repulsed. "So what you're saying is that I should get remarried, stay home, and do some other fool's laundry. You've got a lot of nerve, lady." Marguerite stepped into the street, craned her neck to get a better view, standing right in the way of the older woman, looking for the bus.

"You're just like my mother. But at least she has enough sense to keep her mouth shut. All she does is inhale and hold it whenever I'm around now. It's maddening. Then she'll exhale really slowly, like it's all some impossible effort to just be around her own daughter." She kicked a double-A battery into the storm drain and stepped back on the sidewalk. "No offense, but doing some guy's laundry doesn't preserve his dignity or keep him from being a fool. It just makes me one."

"No one is a fool at my house."

"What does he do for you?"

"What business is that of yours what he does, or what I do, for that matter?"

Marguerite pressed on. "See? That's exactly what I thought you get out of it. Nothing. Not today. Not tomorrow. Not a year ago April. Not ever. That's why you don't see me doing any asshole's laundry. They're all the same."

"They certainly are not. The assholes are completely different from the fools. And none compare to those blessed rat bastards."

Marguerite at first refused to laugh, but then softened, suddenly letting the corners of her mouth turn up—another inevitable dawn—and laughed loudly. "Yeah. You're right about that. The rat bastards are the only ones worth a damn."

The woman with the roots smiled slightly.

They both saw the bus coming. It was several blocks away, but they began to gather themselves.

Marguerite—uplifted in spite of herself—went on. "It's not my business. I don't care, why would I? But it's an important question. Consideration? Love? Respect? Gratitude? What do you get out of it for all your diligent housework? Your cooking, cleaning, grocery servitude."

Silence. The older woman exhaled. The breath was forcibly controlled.

Marguerite flared up again. "I'll tell you what you get. You get what I got: two kids who hate you, one who stood stunned and watched you—actually saw you—smash a car windshield with a trumpet case. Well. I'm sorry. I was enraged. I don't give a shit that they were sleeping together. It was that woman—I don't know. It was a lot of things but mainly it was how she stood there on my front step smirking like she'd won some Olympic laurel wreath when all she got is the sorriest excuse of a man. I just lost it. Couldn't believe she had the nerve to park in my driveway, like she had some right to the place. I don't think so. But, okay, maybe I shouldn't have broken her windshield in front of my kid. I get that. It wasn't my finest hour. But it's the only thing I ever did wrong. Look at everything the two of them did, for how long? So now? In this new relationship? I want the worst, right upfront. Get it over with. Because I know it's coming."

"You don't know that."

"The hell I don't. Let me tell you something. In that courtroom? Do you know what was on that wall? It's ridiculous, it's so outmoded. This mural of Lady Justice in all her reserved manner. Look. Even you, wearing that necklace. It's some saint, not her. That's what I'm talking about. She's got no currency."

"At Daley Plaza?"

The e-cigarette came out again and then disappeared right back into the purse after a quick puff. "No. West. He moved out of the city to be with that whorebag. Filed there. I have to commute for all the custody business. So this courtroom mural? I tell you what, I about went through that window with that damned archaic symbolism up on the walls. Who needs to be confronted with all that? When I'm losing everything I'm supposed to care about I really don't need to be likening myself to Lady Justice, especially not while my kids are at his mom's during this court date. Why isn't there some male model of moral authority up there? Why doesn't he have to deal with all that circumspect pressure, iconography everywhere imposing guilt trips? But. Nope. He's exempt, just completely self-satisfied. Oh I could kill him. I couldn't even look at him. So okay. I looked at her, standing there in her timeless grandeur. Weighing all this support and opposition, and whatever. Like I need to be thinking about that. We're talking about my kids. Hell, my marriage. Who can ever weigh anything on balance? It's just there. You underestimate it, you overestimate it, and you fuck it up. I'm not saying I want to be like Lady Justice but why else is that mural there? It's some ideal, right? We're supposed to aspire to it? How? The scales tip, shit goes out of whack, and then you're fumbling with the whole thing. Chains clanging against each other, weight slamming the thing down. I mean, what is that? Plus, you can't even see what you're doing because of the damn blindfold. So. Okay. Fine. You rip the blindfold off, drop the sword, start scrambling with the weighing pans that have fallen out of the thing. You've got the weights rolling around, bouncing everywhere, and the stuff of perceived value—where is that? Hell. What is that? Cocaine? Gold? What'd you expect? Whatever it is, is dumped out, making a mess everywhere. Then what? You're down on your hands and knees like a jackass trying to make it right. But how are you going to do that? Everything's dropped another ten feet down because you're fucked on a pedestal? How are you going to get down from there? The whole side of the pedestal is covered in the dust that you dropped. All you can do is stand up, brush your robes off if you're lucky, recover your sober sense of decorum, maybe even put the blindfold back on. But the scales are empty. She's always standing there with empty scales. That's bullshit. What is she doing? Nothing. Like you. Right now. Just sitting there staring at me through those sunglasses, completely impassive. What are you weighing out? I don't even care, it doesn't matter. Because you know what? When it comes right down to it I don't want to take the good with the bad, deal with all the better and worse. I want the worst, only. And I want it now—get it over with."

There was no way to say anything, or even to

listen. The older woman looked up to a grand residential building where window washers would make their descent in the not-so-distant future. April would come surely, and diffuse clouds would move through the blue sky on a warmer day above their never seeing each other again. She said nothing. Then ventured to defuse the situation with, "It's good weather at least, while we wait."

"No it's not. It's freezing. And we've waited long enough!"

"It's just the bus, dear."

"What? You were talking about the weather."

The old woman picked up the business card from the bench, read it aloud again. "Tell me about this."

Marguerite wasn't satisfied. It wasn't enough. She said, "I'll be damned if I'd ever do anything again for that rat bastard. A good marriage doesn't just spontaneously exist like some Betty Crocker batch of brownies, just crack one egg and add a third of a cup of oil. That's the childish part of these guys. They think they don't have to help with that shit. They just stand there with Freud pointing fingers, thinking Mommy's supposed to do it all for them. Well. Maybe mothers are the ones who do all the spontaneous existence and the miracles. But, sorry, your wife is the one who needs a little help to build a protectorate for your kids. They expect women to provide these emotional refuges just the way we expect them to provide the actual house. How? And frankly, why? If I'm supposed to help pay the mortgage now? Help staple-gun the fascia under the eaves and then shingle the whole place? Cedar shakes? That gets expensive. If I'm doing all that, then he damn sure better help build us an emotional refuge. It doesn't just miraculously appear. Jesus. And I don't want some shitty emotional lean-to in the woods. Something nice. Something we actually want to live in. You know why? Because I want things too. I want to get tickled, tantalized, mesmerized and doomed, ravished, revealed, fucked, romanticized and ruined. I don't want to be all somber and reserved weighing out right and wrong, like Lady Justice on her pedestal with her scales. So. I'm sorry. But I am not going to commit to someone who can't appreciate this stuff and won't create a construct for us to live in together. There is the physical shelter that a couple needs—the reality. The freaking roof cannot be a leaky caving-in mess. He never dealt with anything. We didn't even get to the point of having gutters to clean but I know he wouldn't have bothered. But I've been in therapy for four years now; there is also that emotional and psychological construct. It has to be there. Two people have to build it. So I swear to God the next time I go into a courtroom they'd damn well better have updated some of these images. Scales? Now? Push a button for the tare. You get a digital readout. And that's it! It's accurate. You know exactly what you've got, how much it weighs. There's no waiting for the torsion balance to quit shifting. No one has to wear any blindfold. There are definitely no brass chains swinging, weighing pans dropping everywhere, clattering."

The older woman waited for her to calm down, to stop fidgeting with the tight waistband of her skirt. She took her wallet from her purse and put the business card inside. Once the pomposity in Marguerite's posture had drained and she looked a little less like a wild animal backed into a corner the woman asked, "Did you ever really want to be married?"

"I don't have to explain my life to you, lady." Marguerite twisted her skirt, folded the waistband over, ripped out the tag that had apparently been scratching her back. Silence. She ferociously chewed one acrylic manicured nail.

NORMA L.

The farm road ended somewhere not too pretty, though sometimes lit well by the rising and setting of the sun. That road got a handful of people home. It could kill your suspension if you weren't careful there where that low-bid oiled rectangle dropped down off a silent section of county highway. After that dip it was one of those head-straight-into-the-horizon roads that made a right angle around an old abandoned brick schoolhouse, and then again at a hog farm. A country graveyard nestled itself between corn and Queen Anne's lace, right at an S-curve. The best part of the drive was where it rose over a weedy sunset-drenched hump of railroad tracks overgrown with royal catchfly and milkweed.

Only two or three people made the drive, downshifting as much for control as to be respectful of the neighbors, crunching gravel slowly enough to hear mourning doves and the pleas of song sparrows piercing bluejoint beard grass. That little road's last stretch ended right in the shadow of a brick-faced duplex, apartments one on top of the other. Parked there under a few isolated oak trees on the final muddy mossy pitch were two cars: a black matte Corvette and a light blue Buick four-door. That Buick must have just been washed. It had those polish circles. The Corvette—God—that Corvette sat covered in three years of oak bits and dust motes.

It was a little after eight o'clock at night. Under a yellow bulb, a door lit by reflected moth wings led into the lower apartment. Over on the side of the building, in an even deeper shadow, an old wet set of wooden stairs rose up to Norma L.'s apartment.

She was sixty-two, had quit smoking but it didn't seem to matter. Emphysema, COPD, hacking cough— airways always acting up in July's heat and humidity. On this night it wasn't too bad, not so much tree pollen in the air. But she was fine to just sit at her dinner table waiting. She'd prepared dinner, nicer than usual for their wedding anniversary, and she stared at a brass candlestick. It was vibrating. She tried to ignore it. She remembered pleasant things seen and done, but those vibrations kept her in the present. She willed herself to concentrate lovingly on her favorite great aunt who had given them the candlesticks as a wedding present.

She hardly could.

The phone rang and in another of their thirty-eight years' of every-evening phone calls someone more than familiar said, "Almost home, sweetie. Had a spill right as I was leaving."

She said almost nothing to him, definitely didn't say a word about the boy downstairs playing his loud music again. She set the phone back down—it was always right there by her elbow—and ignored the vibrations of the candlestick like she ignored her irritation at the music's effect on a pleasant summer evening, ignored magazine covers and headlines about kids, valiant maybe, but just kids. Ignored it all.

She picked up the worn deck of playing cards that was always by her other elbow now that the ashtrays weren't there. She laid out a tableau for solitaire and turned her mind backwards. Back on an old white dress that was still hanging in the cedar closet. Back to a pair of real silk pantyhose that had been the wrong size. Back to nervous, unwrinkled hands holding on to each other at an altar. She flipped the playing cards, scooping one up with another, laying another down on top. She opened the years and arranged them beginning with the ace in ascending order in her mind. But memories didn't hold her interest long. What good were they? Her fingers moved out to the base of the rattling candlestick.

He was so angry, this kid downstairs. He was just nothing but spite and rage now, and who could blame him? But. God. It's not how he'd been. The chair vibrated. And her elbows vibrated where she leaned on the table. Her chin vibrated where she leaned her chin in her hands.

Standing in the open doorway, having overcome the stairs, her husband said, "He's at it again, huh?"

"For two hours."

Mr. L. came in but was already distracted, bent over, fixing the kind of little striped rug so often defeated by the opening of doors. "Well I was going to say there was a spill, which would have been my excuse to make it to the florist and get here just a few minutes late. But then there really was a spill, and so I had to clean that up, before I got over to the florist. They were closed so I had to go around back and pound on the loading dock door. Frank understood. And he already had that bunch ready for me anyway, and I had cash for him. But we talked for a few minutes. Maybe ten. All told, it made me more than late. So. I'm sorry." This was all explained to the floor and the arrangement of the little rug. Turning to his wife Mr. L. said, "Happy anniversary." He tried not to yawn as he handed her a white and pink bouquet, mainly tulips.

Moving across the old linoleum, he forgot to kiss her and was already lifting pot lids on the stove—sniffing at the mashed potatoes, poking broccoli with a nearby fork—and snooping in the oven to see how the roast was coming. It was done. Just resting there, waiting for him. "Smells good, Mom."

Their kids were scattered. Two of them had called dutifully first thing in the morning, made a point of it, put their own kids on the phone and all that. The third barely knew his own birthday let alone his parents' anniversary. It was fine. Maybe they'd all be there for the fortieth. Norma didn't care too much for big events like that though. She hated having to justify plane tickets and rental cars. She'd say, "Just come." They didn't ever hear it. So she stopped saying it. This kid downstairs was between the ages of their children and grandchildren. They had enjoyed getting to know him over the past ten years, probably mattered more than he should.

Mr. L. stood in the middle of the room vibrating himself, then making a little joke of it, exaggerating it head-to-foot. He looked at his wife (who resisted giving him a smile) and said, "I could go down and say something to him."

"Don't you dare. You've got no right. He pays his rent, and you're not his daddy."

"Fine. 'Cause those stairs nearly killed me just now. My knees are—well, what we should have done was rent the top out too and just move into town."

"Affects the taxes."

The cicadas were still going.

"Well those stairs are taxing me half to death. It was one thing with us on the bottom and the kid up here. But between his god-awful ugly choice of posters on the wall, hung so low on the walls they breaks my heart, and those stairs, I just don't know how long this arrangement'll hold up. What are we gonna do when the stairs freeze? You want a new hip for Christmas?"

"Don't think that way. Those stairs are doing you a service. You've lost at least five pounds. Good for your heart."

"It's good for my memory too. 'Cause I'll tell you. I don't forget anything in the truck anymore. I sit there thinking long and hard about what needs to go up, and I take what of it I can carry. If I do end up forgetting something? Forget it."

She laughed. "Stop, you old crank. I've made you a nice dinner, now, and the least you can do is sit down and enjoy it."

"Need a shower or I won't feel right. I know you've been waiting. Will she keep another twenty minutes?"

"She'll have to."

He was gone.

She opened the green tissue paper and cut the three rubber bands. Free, the greenery rolled over itself on the drain board. Tulips thick-folded in their own leaves tried not to bloom just yet. Lanky rose stems seemed unnatural stripped of their thorns. The sweetness of the lily of the valley offered a little relief. She cut stems to fit her favorite vase while her feet vibrated from the kid's music. She sighed and hesitated with scissors opened around a thick stem, the water running. Her eyes filled with tears—why did it have to be him?—and she cut the stem as quickly as she could.

But then she'd done it and gasped, overtaken by how easy it was to slice right through. She left the rest of the stems alone. The bouquet was like a staircase half the right height and half too tall.

Norma L. didn't want to see this young man as fragile as a flower stem. She wanted to believe what he believed about himself, what he'd gone off with, that invincibility.

Giving up arranging, she sat down and stared at the television. The couch vibrated. Mr. L. came out from the tiny bathroom dressed nicely and stood near the television combing his hair. He pulled out his shirt and re-tucked it, loosening the belt one notch. He was vibrating.

Pretended not to be.

Mrs. L. used her favorite old lighter on the candles and ambled over to the wall switch. The blue evening outside seemed so calm compared with the downstairs racket. She flipped off the overhead light and came back to the dinner table slowly, forgetting to look her husband in the eye.

He didn't care. He pulled out the chair for his wife. She sat down and smoothed a napkin across her lap. Mr. L. patted her shoulders with both hands and kissed the top of her head. "My blue-eyed bride."

Norma didn't say anything about cataracts or glaucoma, let him have his romance for the moment.

He stood behind her and yawned, then sat down next to her, tented his fingers, and looked at the flowers. "Seems like Frank does a nice job, but, sorry, I guess I should have got there before the shop closed. This bunch looks all cockeyed somehow."

"Frank did not sell you cockeyed flowers. I just only cut half the stems to fit the vase."

"Why not cut them all?"

It was that unfortunate truth about their neighbor, the one split second that changed his whole life. But she didn't admit it. It wasn't like any of them would be trooping down any proud parade route with the Knights of Columbus. "I just couldn't."

Mr. L. suppressed another yawn but didn't ask his wife for further explanation. He knew it was the kid's whole ordeal. "Yeah."

The candlesticks vibrated on the table. Light danced on the ceiling. They sat without serving each other. Norma said, "He's always up. I read about it. It's called hyperarousal."

"I'll show you hyperarousal."

It was like he hadn't even said it. She mused on, "It's a part of it. Can't sleep. Can't concentrate. Always on the lookout, like something's about to happen. Damn scared animal under the gun. Probably wasn't a fan of Fourth of July, fireworks and that." She touched the tiniest flower on the lily of the valley. "Remember Aunt Ginny?"

"Yeah. She was something. Good Christian."

"Nobody ever knew it."

"Best kind."

"Yeah." She laughed again. There they were, those flowers. "So you thought Frank sold you some bum arrangement for my anniversary, huh? He wouldn't dare. He'd be out of business quick. Anniversary flowers is about all he does sell. And funeral flowers, I guess. But

Lord, it's not quite time to start saving money for those."
She got caught in the sweetness and hell of seeing the kid
half cut down in the bouquet. "What were you going on
about with that Viagra commercial you were auditioning
for a minute ago?"

This time it was like she hadn't even said it.

"Some things can't be helped. The spill held me
up."

She said, "You tired?"

"Might just be the heat. Shower helped."

They sat together with their memories of those
years, each of them staring at a vibrating candlestick.

At some point the cicadas had stopped.

"We've been through more than our share
together, wouldn't you say, Mom?"

"More than a bit." Norma swept the deck of
cards into her hands again, just her habit to hold
something after years of cigarettes.

The ceramic salt and pepper shakers on the back
of the stove vibrated.

"Mom," Mr. L. was cautious. "I could ask him for
an hour. It's your anniversary. You deserve to have some
peace in your own home."

"And he doesn't?" The moths by the downstairs door swirled around the aluminum-shaded bulb. Aspirants of their kind bumped up against the upstairs windows. "He's just a kid."

"Don't I know that much? But I'm just an old man. And you're just an old woman."

"I'm not just anything."

They laughed.

She picked up his plate to begin serving. They looked at each other and vibrated. She put the plate back on the table and stood. Her husband took her by the hand, walked her to the door, and they made their way slowly, one in front of the other, down the damp mossy set of outside stairs. They stood at the bottom looking at the oak trunks in the last bit of daylight.

Norma pointed toward the flat spot of the drive. "Thanks for washing my car."

"Wasn't quite warm enough for the wax. Streaked some. But she still looks good between his sorry old Vette and my beat-up old truck."

"That Vette's not old at all."

"It's looked a hell of a lot better than it does now."

"Maybe you could wash it for him. Take it and get it cleaned up a bit."

"Not until he asks me to. Not my place. And even if he does it might not run."

"It'll run." She knew it would. It had to. Before he went overseas the kid had been so much more than their neighbor, always checking on them, telling them some crazy stories from work, never once making it seem like he was doing a couple of old people a favor, just a friend looking out, checking in. And now what? He wasn't even twenty-two and his biggest fears were just like theirs, blood clots and curtailed independence. Blackness surrounded them now, except where the moths swarmed. She reached her free hand up into the swirl of soft wingbeats. Moths avoided her. Disappointed, she dropped her hand, looked at the Corvette's curves again. "He did drive that thing crazy, didn't he?"

"What a fool he was. Remember when he drove it right into that old cemetery? When was that?" Mr. L. laughed.

Norma laughed too. Mr. L. retold the familiar story at the edge of the moth light. "Five years. Must be at least. God. Wait. Maybe only three. So much has happened. Whenever it was, here he came running up the lane and just pounding on that door there shouting. 'Mr. L., get the winch. Get the winch and bring the dually!'"

That night of outstripped limits, innocence, and shock roared back to their hearts. Mr. L. went on. "He was scared shitless. Hadn't had a thing to drink. Just took that gravel corner too quick, and don't you know he cleared the ditch completely, he told me, and ran that damned Vette all into that old pack of graves."

Mr. L. had joyful tears in his eyes reliving it. "I got the winch and the dually and you were out there in your rollers with the deer light. Remember, Mom?"

She was smiling and nodding.

"I'll never forget that kid's face. He loved that car and he was just trying to figure out how to get the chain on the fender to pull it out. He couldn't do it at all. Shaking so hard. I had to do it for him. Remember? Oh Lord, what a night. And remember after all that, the three of us looking at those gravestones after we finally got the car out on the road? Remember?"

Norma L. took over the story, "Don't I ever. We were so concerned getting the car out I don't think it crossed our minds about those headstones. But his face when he realized it? Oh my God."

Mr. L. reclaimed the story. "He just started pulling up those damned stones trying to put them to rights."

"Wouldn't have mattered. That marble with the burnt rubber tire tracks on it would have stood out more standing up than laying down anyway."

"But he did try his damnedest, didn't he?"

"He's a good kid."

"I know." The lines of the bark on the oak trunks disappeared into the night.

"Remember him that next week?"

Norma L.'s snickering broke into a raucous reaction. She leaned against the house from laughing so hard. "Him talking his way out of trouble at that historical society meeting. I will never forget that. All dressed up. Where'd he ever find that tie he was wearing anyway?"

"I never did know. It wasn't mine. He probably went and bought it special. He's just as proper as they come."

"Except when he's plowing down gravestones."

"Yeah. Except then. But remember that historical society panel—like a damn congressional hearing that was. That poor boy just trying to make it right."

"Just nodding away. Yes sir. No ma'am. So proper."

"I think he volunteered hisself for about a thousand hours of community service too."

"Worked half of them in that patch of gravestones. I've never seen so many holly bushes planted in such a small plot."

"Yeah? Where'd he get all those? And the bulbs. How many damned paper whites does one cemetery need?"

"Not that many. That's for sure."

They straightened up and didn't try to point out stars to one another through the oaks' leaves. Instead they wrapped their arms around each other's waists and approached the first floor door together. They didn't want to be in the moth light. They wanted a more covered and concealed route to the entryway. Mr. L. pulled out a little LED flashlight on his keychain and drew a heart on the kid's door with the light. Norma L. leaned her head on her husband's shoulder, still remembering how earnest the kid was through it all.

Mr. L. squeezed his wife and knocked loudly on the vibrating door.

The stereo clicked off. The stairs stopped vibrating. Quiet spread out over blue bean fields, turning into sustenance somehow. Mr. and Mrs. L. couldn't quite hear the moth wings lighting the doorway, with their interminable soft, beating radiance.

Inside, the kid maneuvered to the door. They heard him coming. They braced themselves. The trees merged into the sky as the day's last blue drained away. There were metal noises on the other side of the door. Mr. L. shut his eyes, letting the darkness merge with him as well. And Norma L. smiled a sort of hesitation and hoped the moths weren't too near her hair.

The door opened and Mr. L.'s eyes caught right up.

He said, "Hey, kid. Want a bite to eat?"

The kid backed his wheelchair out of the doorway, inviting them in. They came through and positioned themselves at either side of the entrance. Mr. L. stepped further inside, looking left and right, scanning the room. He stooped down a bit, swept his flashlight beam across the floor for the kid's cat to chase. He shined the light in the far corners of the room, pointing out the changes for his wife without the kid even knowing.

Norma L. stood firm with her back to the wall. She kept her gaze high, picked up what her husband indicated to her with the seemingly meaningless cat-play. He'd already assessed the familiar size and shape of the room. Her philodendron on top of the refrigerator had died. She was careful not to pepper the kid or her husband with nervous chatter.

She provided immediate security. "It's our—well, we just haven't had a chance to cook for you since you've been back. We thought tonight was as good a night as any. You like pot roast?"

"Pot roast? I knew it. Smelled it all afternoon cooking. Some kind of celebration dinner, huh? Thought it was Mr. L.'s birthday. But it's a surprise for me?"

Norma nodded.

"Thanks. Thanks a lot, Mrs. L." The kid looked at his stereo and then shifted in his chair. "Does my music ever bother you guys?"

"Not at all. I don't even hear it." She turned to her husband, "Do you ever hear it, dear?"

"Nope. This is an old building. Sturdy. Not thin walls like these new places."

They'd gained the foothold.

Mr. L. turned off his flashlight, dropped it back into his pocket.

She forced a smile. Finding that ineffective, she raised her eyebrows to enforce some kind of brightness on her face. She looked at the kid. "Do you mind if I set up the table?"

"Come on in. You know where everything is. It's your house."

They moved toward the table. The kid said, "I'm trying not to nick it, it's so pretty. I stay away from it with the chair. I'm still not a pro in this thing."

Mr. L. put his hand on the speaker that had been reverberating the whole place. He pushed it away from himself to read the label, let it go, let it fall back into place, and said, "Don't worry about the table, kid. It's old as can be. It can take a few lumps." He picked up a 9-volt battery with a little green piece of plastic on top. He said to the kid, "What's this?"

"It's a Phoenix Beacon. It's for covert marking and positive identification in a hostile environment. The beam can't be seen with the unaided eye. You need a night vision device. Someone clipped it to my ruck."

Mr. L. pressed it a few times. "Is it on?"

"Maybe." The kid said, "Might have saved my life."

Down the hall, in the linen closet, Mrs. L. found her own mother's favorite tablecloth still folded carefully on an upper shelf. She forgave the disorder on the lower shelves, where wrinkled towels, half-used bottles of cologne and well-worn earphones were piled in an accessible jumble behind that small door. Back in the room, smiling self-consciously, she spread out the tablecloth, made several trips up and down the stairs, bringing each dish in turn. The men talked. And since the young man couldn't offer much assistance they concentrated on other proper things in conversation and pretended it was okay not to help with carrying the dishes down those wet wooden stairs. Mrs. L. made the trips on her own, in her low navy pumps.

The men hovered as Mrs. L. arranged the table. Mr. L. was careful not to block the entrance. The kid said, "It's so sweet. I wish I could finish something like that. Walnut?"

"Maple."

Mrs. L. set the flowers in the middle of the table. She wished she had finished arranging them, hated their being two heights. It had been his legs that kept her from cutting the other half of the stems. Those scissor blades around the living things just could not close. But now, God, she wished she had. She couldn't bear looking at the disparity, hurried to leave again, and let one moth in by accident.

Mr. L. covered for her quickly. "My daddy made that table. I was a kid. Helped him with some of the finishing work. A lot of love in it."

The kid lifted the tablecloth and ran his hand across the wood. "Maybe I could do that. Make furniture or something."

"Sure you could. That garage is half workshop already. We could make a boardwalk through the oaks over to it. Wouldn't take a weekend to do that. I've seen plenty of boardwalks in state parks now. Makes 'em accessible. I'm sure the plans are online. You could help me figure it."

"I've never really done anything with wood. Just cars or whatever. But it's hard to lean under the hood now. You know? So maybe wood. Pull it onto my lap, right?"

"Yep. You're young yet. Plenty of time to learn."

Mr. L. swallowed hard. He still had the Phoenix Beacon in his hand, had been fiddling with it without even realizing it. The kid indicated it with a nod. "It's got an encodable transmitter on it." Mr. L. tossed the thing into a coffee mug full of loose change. At the sound, the kid's cat jumped up onto the little end-table, stuck its nose into the mug, then hopped back down and zipped away to focus fully on that one moth bumping against the ceiling.

Mrs. L. came back with more serving dishes, and took off pieces of foil.

The kid pulled up and slammed his chair against the wood by accident. "I'm so sorry."

"What'd I say, kid?"

Norma said, "The tablecloth will keep it from marking. Don't worry about it, honey. Hand me your plate."

The kid gave them the best of what was left of his own smile. He handed her his plate. As she returned it and both their hands were on it, he said, "It happened in Mosul."

Norma L. let go.

Mr. L. said, "Well, you're home now." Hand on

the nearest shoulder.

The cock-eyed flowers, the Phoenix Beacon, the moth, Mr. and Mrs. L. and the kid filled up the room before retracting .

The kid fidgeted with the wheelchair brake. "Your candlesticks are real pretty Mrs. L."

"Thank you. They were a wedding gift from my Great Aunt Ginny."

"Yeah?"

"Yeah."

"How long you guys been married?"

"Thirty-eight years tod—thirty-eight years."

"Wow. That's a long time."

The kid put the napkin in his lap. Mrs. L.'s eyes filled with tears. She stared hard at the flowers, forcing her tears into submission. She smiled pleasantly but had to convince her eyebrows to pull everything up hopeful again as she did her best to keep her mind out from under the table. She didn't want to be confronted by that contemptible truth of his wheelchair.

The kid said, "I'm sorry you gotta climb those stairs now, Mr. L. I know your knees are bad."

"My knees are just fine. And it's good for the

heart, kid." He looked down at his plate, took up his knife and fork, sat up as straight as he could, leaned in, gave a quiet-quick wink to his wife, and cut the pot roast.

HOW TO CHERISH THE GRIEF-STRICKEN

Libi, her best friend and neighbor two doors over, really did try to forgive Terese. It was Libi who went to see her prior to her arraignment.

It had definitely been an accident. But there was no doubt Terese reversed right into that tree, slammed on the gas for some reason, killed both her kids on impact, broke all their facial bones. She and her husband Jim had smartly opted to save money on the used minivan so they could put the difference in the girls' college fund. The older van didn't have the easy-to-latch car seat docks. But that wasn't what did it. Terese had had too much wine for the officer to ignore. At first in her panic, coursing with adrenaline, she had refused the breathalyzer, then she'd demanded to take one, convinced she was under the limit.

Whichever year it was—2011—no, 2012—Libi's first visit to Terese was on December 19th. Gessica, Libi's daughter, had rushed into the kitchen where her mother stood at the sink in a thick chenille robe, its applique ice cream cones aging to threadbare. Libi's eyes were puffy from an exhausting bout of uncontrollable tears.

She was only going two blocks.

Years of Libi's suppressed jealousy had ended instantly with one short gasp when Connie called with the news. "They're dead, Lib. Both of them." "Who?" "Terese did it." "Did what?" "Gessica's fine. She's here with us. Just come." "Where?" Connie—of course it was Connie who called—had hung up without elaborating. Libi was almost the last of their friends to show up. Everyone assumed she'd seen the accident or at least heard the emergency response vehicles. It all basically happened right in front of her house. When they were all convening at the hospital with Jim, Connie leaned over to this woman Marie and whispered, "Does Libi even know?" Marie motioned for her to move further away, out of Jim's earshot. "Mall-walking. She dropped Gessica off at the sleepover right when I was coming back with Hannah's box of beads. Lib said she was going to see a movie and then put six thousand steps on her pedometer."

Terese and Jim were the friends who had pulled her back to life, got her going to church with them after such an embarrassing divorce. When Warren left, replacing him was the last thing on Libi's mind. She certainly wasn't after anyone else's man. It was ridiculous how many women were threatened with her around. Terese hadn't been. She trusted Jim and Libi. It meant a lot. Libi had appreciated their efforts but still hadn't wanted to be happy and got sick of doing the right thing all the time on behalf of her daughter, and them. She'd resented a lot at the time: Jim and Terese with their perfect house, perfect marriage, perfect kids—those two sweet girls.

Now? It had been four days. Libi sipped coffee in silence and looked out at her tilted mailbox post.

Gessica's little warm body pressed entirely against

her mother's leg, her head leaning on the curve of Libi's hip. Three angels descending hung there in the window without any sunlight to scatter across the room. The girls had made the suncatchers in Sunday school. Maybe Libi should take one to Terese, she thought. The one that still had its halo.

Libi reached out and took down the angel. Its metal edges clinked against the glass. She held it, ready to wrap it in tissue, maybe find a gift bag, but then she remembered how all the girls had insisted the three angels must stay together at Libi's house in a window where Terese could see them all the time. Because of the shape of the street and the size of the houses the two women had a direct line of sight kitchen-to-kitchen. It hadn't mattered then. She and her friend were just two mothers keeping the peace that day. They appeased their dictatorial children, hurrying to find suction cup hooks and matched lengths of nearly invisible fishing line.

Libi put the angel back.

Beyond the suncatchers, she looked at where the tree had been cut down. That one blasted tree.

The logs, covered in a thin layer of ice, were stacked neatly in the gutter. But who could blame Jim?

It wasn't his fault. Libi put herself right in that driver's seat with Terese. She felt her body loosen and then clench in the torture, braced herself before impact, imagined having her own seat belt on, for not even ten seconds, not even five, for one maybe, a fraction even.

She couldn't take it. They'd just made those damn angels, just hung them up, not even two weeks ago. How do you cherish the grief-stricken? It was impossible to give up Terese's daughter, little Lulu, with her two mini bobby pins and her one-inch wispy pony tail sticking straight off her nape, with her headband, her little determined face, her grownup black cardigan—one button closed at the collar—with her hard seeking eyes. And Kat. Oh sweet Kat. Those lanky legs in white tights.

Libi's stomach turned over, and she felt nauseated as she stroked Gessica's silken hair. Libi dreaded the duty but would leave in about an hour. "I'll only be gone until six."

Gessica pulled on a hand towel. It was attached to the oven handle with a crocheted loop. The maroon yarn stretched and contracted with each little-girl tug. "But

Mommy, where are you going?"

"You know where I'm going. We talked about it."

"Are you taking sunflowers?"

"No. I'm not taking sunflowers."

"But Terese likes sunflowers."

No more perfect marriage, no more little pink cheeks and Scotch plaid at Christmas. No more red velvet ribbons in those little girls' hair, with the dog in the picture. That damned Labrador retriever wearing a huge brass jingle bell on a complementary green velvet collar. Terese even had Kat and Lulu in pinafores once.

They really were good friends, not associated only by proximity and convenience. They had laughed, gossiped, helped each other hang Christmas lights on their eaves. Jim went up the ladder while Libi untangled lights and Terese hovered around the base of the ladder, assuring the symmetry of scalloped garlands. Even so, Libi used to mutter her judgments into a bottle of pinot grigio, while doing lackadaisical leg-lifts from her glass-topped coffee table. One, two, forget it. *Where'd she even get pinafores?* Three, four, fine. *Probably hundreds of dollars each and imported.* Five, six, flip the channel. Libi would point her toe, flex her glutes, drink, and mumble to herself about what kind of sappy person dresses her kids like twin Raggedy Ann dolls.

Never again.

How many times had they all been in that minivan?

Somehow, the kitchen floor did not buckle. Jim had installed it for Libi last summer. It was laminate, a high-resolution hardwood photograph, really, under a plastic finish. Spalted maple still newly smooth at the joined pieces. Gessica's sock-toes traced a tight crack, maybe just a little mad, maybe just a little wanting to break a mother's back.

"Goldie will stay with you all morning. You're going to make snowflakes, to go with the angels."

The little girl knew to not quite whine but yet she voiced her protest. "But I always go where you're going."

What could she say? "Some places are only for adults."

"Like broker stock offices?"

Libi refused to add sex shops, strip clubs, and couldn't say jail. "I'm going to visit Kat and Lulu's mommy."

"Because she was a bad mommy?" Yet it seemed

even Gessica couldn't follow through on such a harsh judgment. This was a woman who had put pink lemonade frosting on confetti cupcakes for her. "She's not bad, Mommy. I went in the car with her lots of times. Rollerskating. Swimming. Dance lessons. Soccer. Church. Six Flags. And nothing ever happened. 'Member? I'll be quiet." The little girl held out the towel so her mother could dry her hands after rinsing the coffee mug. Libi accepted the gesture though the seasonal towel did little to absorb any water. "I know, sweetie."

Gessica's four fingers were through the crochet brass-knuckle style. She was tugging, pulling, sliding her feet back and forth, her whole will, her whole little anxious being, ever solicitous. "So I can come?"

An impatience familiar to them both struck like a cobra. "Quit asking. You're not going this time." Libi hated having to dominate that little strong will. Though a mother was an enforcer, must be, she hurried to modulate the blow. "Want to watch cartoons while we wait for Goldie?"

"You never let me watch TV in the morning. That's the rule. Why are you changing everything?"

For the love of God. These endless negotiations.

In some ways, yes, maybe it would be nice for them to be over, forever. Libi scooped up her daughter and put her on her shoulder. She kissed the little belly that rolled against her cheek. She carried the wriggling, writhing, giggling, little-bit-too-heavy body into the living room and planted it firmly on the microfiber couch under a huge fuzzy blanket.

Libi immediately blocked out her strangely renewed jealousy of Terese, who was undoubtedly free, if damned. Libi found the stuffed bear, Mr. Topkins, on the landing, turned and shouted, "Catch!" The bear arched fast to free fall over the railing, landing ear-first on her daughter.

Upstairs after her shower she put on her robe and wandered over to the window. There was that expanse of asphalt, that curving curb, and the wood, the simple fact of what Jim had felt he had to do to destroy that beautiful old tree after the accident. Terese's husband wasn't controlling in the usual ways. He didn't get jealous, never said she had to be anywhere at any set time, didn't fight with her about what she should do and be. He was like this, always stacking everything, building prisons around them both.

Libi had watched him cut the wood, had stood transfixed two days before. It was a quiet revenge. First he took off what limbs he could reach. Then, remorseless, the whole tree crashed down in the cul-de-sac. One of the upper branches banged against Libi's mailbox, tilting the post. Jim would fix it, she knew that. It wasn't important now. Ridding them all of that tree was what had been necessary. And he'd done that. He was not furious with the chainsaw. There was virtue in how he took that tree apart, steadily, all evening. Libi imagined his two little girls, resistant to the next life, standing right there by him that afternoon. He was so efficient in his work, so gentle even. Maybe each of the girls ran their little ghost fingers along that whirring chain, exactly as they'd stroked newly discovered curves of feathers.

Libi couldn't look at the woodpile anymore. It was too sad. Her eyes darted from one house to another, randomly, avoiding the fact that a light had flipped on in Jim's bedroom. He was so close, so inaccessible. In much the same way that rage had gripped her in that moment downstairs, fear now choked her when she realized she had no salt to melt the ice in the driveway, for Goldie.

For one moment she came undone: she saw Goldie slipping, falling, breaking a hip, an ambulance coming (it would be the same ambulance that had come the other night for the girls, the same paramedics: Libi almost heard them exchanging judgments about the subdivision, the cul-de-sac, the collective negligence, the breakdown of all good things behind the facade of utmost propriety; Jim would see them, would recognize them, would disappear into a deeper part of his hell). Libi flew into an internal fury over Goldie's needing major surgery, then inevitably suing Libi, and ultimately she tormented herself with the prospect of Goldie's demise. It would be her fault that this sweet old woman lay dying in a hospital bed with a blood clot stuck in her lungs; or—no—it would be an aneurysm, or—even worse—she'd bleed out with the blood-thinner dose too high, if she didn't contract pneumonia after aspirating her pudding.

Reason returned, though it was an effort to breathe, to find herself in the room again, to come back to life in that safe upstairs bedroom, as on that god-awful morning when they'd all lived but the girls. Libi put herself back together, knowing Goldie would avoid the slick driveway and come straight to the front door across the frozen grass.

And a few minutes later, that was what she did. The doorbell rang. Libi heard her daughter jump up off the couch and run in her socks across the fake wood to answer the door.

Libi couldn't take it—all that vibrant life. She sat down on the end of her bed.

She fell back on the bed, almost wishing her ex-husband were there in his old driving moccasins telling her what to do. This was a time when it might have helped. She lay where her daughter had been conceived seven years ago. Now she remembered the one special fight that had preceded a lot of laughs, enough true love, and their most beautiful way forward into the world. They had both known it would be a girl. Libi rolled over and felt the quilted flowers.

Almost in protest of the past, she got herself up, took off the robe, put on a dress, took off the dress, threw on some comfortable jeans, and found a way to join Goldie and her daughter downstairs in the kitchen where Goldie met her brightly with, "Libi, I hope you won't mind." Several grocery bags were lined up on the counter. "Connie just called. I've been tasked with making four dozen cookies. Gessica's agreed to help."

Libi ran her fingers through her little girl's hair, wondering where the hairbrush might be. She didn't care about cookies. She stared at the angels in the window. "The girls made those together. Do you think I should take one to Terese?"

Children enjoy being heard. Gessica's three fingers made their way through her mother's belt loop. Her pretty little public-display voice said, "We're going to make fumeral cookies and only make snowflakes if there's time."

Libi could not bring herself to say, "Funeral. Not fumeral." She pulled her daughter against her.

"Don't cry today, Mommy. You cried all day yesterday."

"Where's your apron, sweetie? And Goldie needs one, too. Don't you think?"

The little girl nodded and ran over to the middle drawer to pick out two special aprons.

Goldie said to Libi, "I don't know what they'd do about stained glass angels. They'll confiscate scissors or any of that, I'm sure. Even nail clippers." She paused, then said more insistently, "You should lock your whole purse in the trunk. You don't want to have to think about what might be in it."

Libi reached out for Goldie's hand, "Jim doesn't want Terese out on bail."

Goldie nodded too quickly.

"Connie's going to take Terese's mom to a law firm at three o'clock." Libi squatted down to her daughter and gave her a huge hug after approving the chosen aprons, one of maroon corduroy caked with flour on the bib from the year before and the other with an applique sprig of holly for a pocket. "I'll be back in a few hours."

When the garage door went up, Libi felt her breathing quicken and the internal spiral started again. Backing out of the driveway was nearly impossible. She knew her daughter was inside, safe. She knew the other kids on the block were older, wouldn't run out in front of her car. But knowing didn't help. She kept her foot on the brake, her eyes on the rearview mirrors, inched and eased the car down the driveway into the cul-de-sac.

It really was too much to even consider visiting Terese. Libi might have given up, quit, but there was that pile of wood. Robust yet flagging: Jim's kind of perfect was almost like the little drummer boy's gift, not enough, but all he had to offer, those saw marks still vivid in the logs.

A sign had been added: *Free wood.*

No one had taken any. Everyone knew the story.

Libi made a mental note to do something about getting rid of that split wood. She'd call friends who didn't know, didn't matter to the situation. There had to be someone who didn't know the meaning of that tree, who could offer real compassion by acting in ignorance, who could be giddy, and greedy, and glad to collect everything down to the bark chips.

At first Libi inched the car forward, barely able to stand the uncontrollable speed of the idle, mailbox by mailbox. Though the way forward to see Terese seemed daunting, she refused to look back, knowing Gessica would be there leaning against the back of the couch, looking out the picture window, waving, willing her back.

Snow had started. Not much. Flurries in the air. A trace on the pavement, blowing in those gorgeous serpentine ribbons. Her windshield fogged up. She pressed a button marked *vent.*

What else could she do?

The world betrayed no one in particular, yet there it was, closing in on her: the Thanksgiving decorations that some vacationing neighbors forgot to take down before they left for Captiva, a new pickup truck parked too far from the curb in a street too small for it, houses with the wrong siding, wrong storm doors, curtains too old-fashioned for energy-saving windows, cheap fencing sealed with whatever stain product must have been on sale. It was all like that, everywhere she looked. Her eyes got no relief until she turned out of the subdivision and headed down a road flanked by undeveloped land for sale.

Advent was supposed to be a time of anticipation, of hoping for salvation. Libi didn't dare. She gripped the steering wheel, leaned forward to wipe moisture off the inside of her windshield.

The first year after Warren, her husband, left had been impossible. She'd had to figure out a day-care situation near her work since his mother ruefully decided not to watch Gessica anymore as she had deemed it a help to Libi and not to her granddaughter.

Never had Libi believed she would stay in the suburbs in a big house. That had not been her plan. But the thought of Gessica in city schools didn't appeal to her either. She just hung on, dug in, did what she could with the house and lawn when she had time. Jim did quite a bit for her as often as he could. Libi never wanted anyone to pick sides though it was satisfying that Jim never again spoke with Warren.

There was no one else, but Libi hated needing Terese and Jim so much. Terese had taken Libi under her wing when Libi was most vulnerable. She hated the pity related to being divorced, raising a little girl on her own. Hated the apologies, the postures of empathy, the rounds of jolly camaraderie, the patronizing condescension that came from couples who assumed they were exempt. She endured it, knowing how many of them had similar fates ahead. But Terese had never done that. Terese just came over with a bottle of wine after her own kids had gone to bed. Left them with her husband watching ESPN downstairs and walked right through Libi's door, intent on keeping her company on those hellacious nights when it required more than she had to give to assure Gessica had a safe, secure home. Terese sat right down on the couch, poured champagne into lidless sippy cups, and insisted in her inimitable whisper, "They're all assholes."

Terese didn't guard her husband from Libi like the other women had, so savagely insecure. Terese got it and didn't care if her husband smiled at Libi. It was Jim who finally got Libi to laugh after six months of their barbecues, carpools, and church. They'd risen to every occasion. It was unthinkable that Terese was locked up, facing a lifetime of self-loathing.

Libi couldn't take it. She pulled into the parking lot of a pizza place. Who could she call for consolation? She scrolled through her contacts. Her mom wouldn't be up yet. Warren might be. He wasn't that much of an asshole, just busy all the time. She inadvertently called him but hung up before she got a connection. He'd be heading to some airport. It wasn't worth getting into the whole thing over the phone, it was too much. She'd tell him once things calmed down. She dialed Goldie's cellphone. "Can I talk to Gessica?"

Her daughter got on the phone. "What, Mommy?"

"Hi, babe. You having fun?"

"With Goldie?"

"Yeah."

"Goldie's looking at bowls. Why're you calling?"

Libi didn't have an answer. "Do you need anything?"

"Mommy, do you need a hug?"

Libi couldn't say a word, not one word. Then, "Yes, baby. I do."

"Come home! I'll give you a hug. Goldie will give you a hug, too. Goldie's good at hugs. She's got a hug-a-monster that comes out from behind the couch. You wanna come back home, play with me and Goldie and the hug-a-monster?"

Libi was only a half-mile away. She could easily turn back. She thought about it. What was ten minutes? But the jail was probably pretty strict with their visitation times. "I do, baby. I do."

"Then come home!"

She needed to get on her way, be there on time. "You think the hug-a-monster will be there at six?"

Her daughter was not pleased. "No. Hug-a-monster has to have his nap in two hours and a bath at six."

"Well. Will you give me a hug when I get back?"

"No. You have to come now if you want a hug."

"Please? It would mean a lot." Libi mock-bargained with her daughter.

"Are you going to be good? The whole time you're gone?" Her daughter affected a scolding tone.

"Yes, dear. Very good. As good as I can be."

"Then of course you get a hug when you get home!"

"Promise?" Libi was glad to slip away into the role reversal.

"Mommy, just go. Goldie put my snack on the coffee table. We're between batches, going to play War."

Libi heard her daughter say to Goldie, "Mommy's going to be good, Goldie. She promised." Then heard her add, "She doesn't need to talk to you, she said we can have our snack right now."

Libi hadn't said that, had maybe wanted to talk to Goldie, didn't really need a six-year-old executive determining anything for her. The phone went dead.

Libi looked up and saw an employee of the pizza place staring at her. It took her off guard. She put the car in gear and pulled out of the parking lot.

She took a right, headed toward the interstate, but she couldn't imagine getting the car up to full speed on the highway. Three more miles down the road she pulled into another parking lot for one of those stores that sold throw pillows. Libi went inside in a bit of a daze, feeling a little disconnected from the place, from her own actions. But it was familiar. She'd been there alone, with Terese, with Gessica, with all their daughters. She walked up and down the aisles. She stopped, aimless. An employee said, "You doing okay?"

It was impossible to relive such a horror and impossible to stop reliving it. Libi looked at this woman, at the rhinestone lanyard. What was she supposed to do, tell her? Just blurt it out like some raving lunatic? No. Libi smiled, nodded, picked up a deeply discounted book of Crock-Pot recipes so the woman would go away. Then she saw a black velvet pillow. It had hand-painted silk on the reverse. Libi grabbed it, clutched it to her chest. This she wanted to take to Terese, this would help. Terese could put it between herself and the cinderblock walls. Would the guards cut the pillow open? Libi didn't know. She pushed the pillow back into its spot on the shelf—it was too expensive anyway—and left the store.

Back in her car, she dialed the number of a friend from work. There was no answer so she had to leave a message. "Hi, Dove. I remember you'd mentioned something about how expensive firewood is getting? A neighbor of mine had to cut a tree down, left all the wood stacked in his drive. It's free for anyone who wants it. You might need to leave it to dry for a season. But it's right there. Have your boys go pick it up. I'll text you the address."

She hung up. Sent the address to her friend. Knew those boys would be dispatched within fifteen minutes. The wood would be gone before she got home.

Relieved, she got a Coke at a drive-thru window, put the address of the jail in her GPS unit, surprised it came right up as a destination the gadget recognized, and got on the interstate. She drove into the city. The county jail wasn't as far away as she'd thought, right at 26th and California. She'd been by the place probably thousands of times, never fully aware of what that low-profile building was.

She thought of the prison with no walls. Where was that? She couldn't remember.

Libi drove up to a security gate and rolled down her window. "Hello. Hi. I'm here to see Terese Menninger."

The guard said, "Back up five feet." It was raining

now, and she guessed he didn't want to come out of the booth to get her license plate number.

Libi was confused. But she turned the news radio off and carefully put the car in reverse and inched it backwards.

The guard took down the plate number and then motioned her forward. "Repeat offender?"

"Excuse me?"

He laughed. "Just kidding. I meant, have you visited here before?"

"No." Libi stared across the parking lot. There was a patch of ice in a dip. "She's my best friend. She has to be terrified."

"It's gonna be fine. If you don't understand something just ask a question. You'll have about a twenty-minute visit. Try not to say too much. Try to listen as much as you can. Sometimes if you say the wrong thing the inmate could take offense and get worked up. So let her talk to you. Okay? Just being here is a big deal. Don't provoke her. Whatever she did, she doesn't need that from you."

"Can I park anywhere?" A text came through from her work friend. *The boys got it all. Thank you!*

"The visitor spaces are over by that ramp. Just go on up and in through that door. Have a good one."

Libi parked, left her purse in the car. Who would break into a car in a jail parking lot? The security inside wasn't such a big deal. She walked through a couple of bolted doors, down a ramp, and sat in a visitation room that was more hospitable than she had imagined. There were paper Christmas decorations on the walls. An old fiber-optic tree warmed up the security guard's booth. She waited behind glass with air holes on a seat bolted to the floor, looked at the gang scratches on the counter: initials, letters, an upside-down crown.

A guard brought Terese into the room.

Libi stood up to hug her but the guard shook her head. Libi sat back down. "Terese! How are you? You look great!"

Terese did not look great. Her hair was washed and combed but flat. Terese always curled her hair. She was dressed in the jail's unflattering uniform. Libi had never seen her without makeup. Terese's eyes shifted over the room and landed, without looking Libi in the eye, on Libi's locket.

Dammit.

There was a new tone in Terese's voice. "Remember that Mother's Day? Was that just last year?"

Libi nodded. She had forgotten to take off the locket. How could she have forgotten? The security guard specifically said not to provoke her.

Terese went on. "Kat must have cut the pictures for the lockets. Lulu and your daughter wouldn't have had hands steady enough. I know Jim didn't do it. Those pictures were only about half an inch across. His fat fingers couldn't do that kind of delicate work. It was Kat, I'm sure of it."

Libi nodded but followed the gate guard's advice and let Terese talk.

"She had that detailed care."

"Like you have."

"Like Jim has. Not me. I thought he took them to the mall or downtown to Schaffer's or something, but he didn't. Jim told me months later that he'd been watching golf. Kat knew I wanted a locket and that you'd want one too and that there was no one to really buy you anything for Mother's Day after—well, forgive me, after that asshole left you. She found those lockets online. And she went and got Jim's wallet after he fell asleep. She talked to the mail lady, got her in on it, had the lady put the box on her window ledge while she was at school, found the right pictures to go inside, wrapped them and everything."

Libi swallowed.

Terese shook her head. She pretended to laugh. She pretended to care. "Then that two-faced husband of mine took all the credit when those gifts came out after church. Remember?"

Libi could barely breathe. "I always thought you bought those for both of us. I loved you for it. It meant so much that year."

"Well I guess Jim took credit for mine. And I took credit for yours. But it was little Kat."

"That means even more."

Libi waited and stared at the Christmas tree with its whispers of love.

Terese asked, "Has Jim told you anything? He won't see me."

Libi hated that this room was below ground level. There were no echoes of mercy. She looked up at the little window above their heads. "Can you have suncatchers? Remember the angels the girls made?" There was no answer. Outside two maintenance women were smoking on their break. Libi watched the bottoms of their shoes scrape the grate over the window.

Terese called her back into the room. "Hey. Libi. I asked you a question? Has Jim told you anything?"

Libi had to answer. It was only fair. "I only know what Connie told me."

"Connie? Why would you listen to her?"

They both laughed. The laughing felt familiar.

Fueled by a moment of their old ease, Libi went on. "Yeah, she's got her nose in everything as usual. Do you want to hear it this way?"

"How else am I going to hear it? Just say it real quick."

Nothing was at rest. "Okay. She said Jim wants to put the house up for sale as soon as he can. That he's going to divorce you. And that he'll probably move near his brother, the one who lives in Riverside."

"Move by Steve? That makes sense I guess."

Libi nodded again, smiling, trying not to shudder. "And he cut the tree down."

"Of course he did. That's what Jim does." There was something in the way she said it, as though she'd been entirely in control the whole time, that she'd known all along. "I'm sure the wood's all stacked perfectly by the house with no twigs anywhere to mess up the lawn mower come summer."

"He left the wood in the street. For people to take."

"Who'll take it?"

Libi didn't tell her. There was no point.

Terese kept staring over to the Christmas tree. "That tree's why we bought the house."

She was mesmerized by the quiet shifting colors of the fiber-optic light. "Jim drinks just as much as I do. You know that. You know it could have been him and not me. You know that."

"I do."

There was no warmth coming from the plastic Christmas tree. Terese said, "But it wasn't. It was me. Because he'd already passed out and the girls kept yanking on me, saying it was time for them to go to the sleepover, insisting that we had to leave. So I took them, you know?"

"I know."

"I'd been worse off and gone further plenty of times."

Libi wished the tinsel swags on the wall hadn't been too heavy for the tape. Several of the swags were secured effectively but then two had dropped and a third was about to. That one would do it, take the whole thing down.

"Jim washed the car seat covers. Said he was sick of looking at how nasty they were. Went to all this trouble. Took them out, pulled the things off. We haven't bothered with that in three years. But he didn't—"

"Didn't what?"

"It doesn't matter." Terese stuck her fingers into the holes in the glass. "I'm pretty sure about most of it until I grabbed those keys. How can I apologize?"

Libi looked up at a paper bell taped to the wall.

"He hates me."

"He doesn't hate you."

"He didn't secure the seats, Lib. He just put the covers back on after he'd cleaned them. Pulled them out to scrub off the clasps, vacuum all the cracker crumbs out from behind them, but didn't deal with weaving the seat belts back through those stupid plastic things." The Christmas tree changed colors.

Libi didn't say a word.

"Libi. It's not possible. I was pulling out of my own driveway. How fast could I have been going? They would have been fine if they weren't in those stupid car seats. They might have been bruised up. Might have tumbled onto the floor in a little undignified heap. But they wouldn't be dead. We were just going a couple blocks, Lib. Do you get that?" Terese started pulling at a strand of her hair, first slowly with a contemplative inattention, then faster, compulsively. "We made the right decision, Lib. I remember him asking if he should do it. He was right to wash those covers. That was the right call. They were nasty. I was so happy he even thought to bother, you know? You know how he is. That's what he does. All that crap. Those seats not being strapped in is not his fault. I've done the same thing to him. When we switch cars, just toss the seats in his backseat without locking them down. Just trying to remember all the logistics. Once the girls get situated, we always give each of them a hug and yank their seats around, to make them laugh, to be sure they're really secure. But I didn't, Lib."

Terese looked up and the two women outside became aware of her, realized she was looking up at their shoes slipping over the window grates. They walked away.

Libi saw their retreat. She waited until Terese turned toward her to say, "I don't know."

Terese started crying uncontrollably. "They just wanted to sleep over at Julianne's house. They were hassling me about it all evening. I didn't want to take them. I knew Lulu would get scared. I knew that Kat would want to stay. I knew that would put Lulu over the edge. I still should have had Lulu stay home. I knew I'd just be going back for her in another hour. And I knew I'd have to make another trip in the morning for Kat. How many times was I really supposed to go around the block that night? It irritated me. That's the truth, Lib. I didn't want to be up half the night with one and then have to get up early in the morning for the other. I could have made them both stay home. But Kat was old enough. She said she wouldn't be scared. She said she should get to be with her friends even if they watched some movie that Lulu wasn't used to. I'd already had I don't know how much wine, Libi. Ten minutes later and I would have been passed out. Kat might have been upset all night, she might have screamed at me the entire next day, but she wouldn't be dead. But somehow I got up and found my keys—I don't know how. It was just a few blocks. Lib, if I'd been thinking at all maybe I could have just walked them over. You know? But it was cold. They had their sleeping bags. I couldn't carry a sleeping bag in the state I was in. Lulu was too little. It would have dragged on the ground the entire way. Would have been soaked. I just got in the van." She reached out to fix the angel tree-topper that had tipped sideways. "Fuck, Lib. Why'd I get in the van?"

"I don't know, See-see."

"That's right, you don't know. Where were you? Why didn't you take them? I always took your kids everywhere. Everywhere. Why couldn't you have taken my girls when you dropped Gessica off?"

"Terese. Stop."

"I'm serious, Libi. Where the fuck were you?"

"Please."

"How many times did I cover for you at school?"

Libi nodded.

"How many times did I have my husband help you at your house when he needed to be dealing with stuff at home?"

Libi said, "I don't know."

"That's right, you don't know shit. You don't

know what it's like to have your own fucking minivan call 911 because it thinks it's so damn smart. You don't know what it's like to have your face smashed in an airbag when you're wasted drunk and have some Pakistani receptionist at Onstar come over the radio and cheerfully tell you that help is on the way! Who has that job anyway? Old-ass used van, but Jim haggled with the dealer to get that bullshit installed. Wanted to protect his kids. Well, you know what? I'm not sure I would have called 911. Because blacked out or not I knew I was loaded. I might just have gone inside and sobered up. But the fucking car that Jim just had to have ratted me out."

"Ratted you out?"

"Yes."

"Terese. Your girls died."

"But I did not kill them, Libi."

Libi said, "I called."

"When?"

"It doesn't matter."

"When did you call?"

"I shouldn't have said anything."

"What are you talking about? When the fuck did you call?"

"Around four."

"To take them over?"

"Yes."

"Why didn't I pick up? Why didn't I know? Why didn't I take your call? Where was I? Where was my phone? Did the call go straight to voicemail? Why didn't one of the girls answer? They always hear my phone."

"I don't know."

"You called?"

"Yes. I wasn't going to tell you."

"But you called?"

"Yes."

"You really called?"

"I did."

"I wouldn't kill my girls, Lib. I didn't do it."

Libi didn't reply. She remembered what the gate guard had said, took a few deep breaths, slowed herself down. Then she said, "Maybe there was ice, Terese. The van's acceleration could have malfunctioned."

"You think that's what happened?"

Libi couldn't look at her. "I'll be back in a week."

"They aren't even going to let me go to the funeral."

"You can't expect Jim to mortgage the house for your bail. Not in a week. It's just all happening so fast. Your mom will be there though. She's staying at Connie's."

"Why Connie's? I hate Connie. Have her stay with you."

"It's all figured out. Connie has that new addition. It'll be fine. She wants to come see you after the funeral."

"Who? Mom?"

"Connie. I can bring your mom next week. But she got in real late last night and wasn't up to coming with me this morning."

"I'm not going to see Connie. I don't care if she does know the chief judge for my assignment. I guess he picks the judge who will—I don't know. Bring Mom. Wait. No. Don't bring Mom."

They were both crying.

Libi got it all out, though. "The service will be in the afternoon at the church. Connie has Goldie making cookies with Gessica today. Pastor Pokorny's coming back from Banff to do the service. The viewing will be tomorrow at the home on Racine Avenue—where your father's was."

Terese was crying so hard that the guard came over and signaled the end of the meeting. "Jim won't know the first thing about planning a funeral. Let alone two of them. Stacking wood, he can do that. But what does he know about coffins for little girls? And headstones. What does he know about any of it? Calling people. Flowers. Renting extra chairs for the house. But don't you dare let Connie determine anything. Have them put something between the caskets at the viewing; I don't know what they even have available for that. Maybe a statue, a pedestal for a flower spray; it's almost Christmas, so something festive, seasonal, holly, spruce, and hypericum if they have any left over—not holly berries— but with something white, something for relief, berries would be fine I guess, or maybe just nothing. Or a palm. That's somber, isn't it? I think so. Get a palm. Tell them to get a palm.

"But that done, decided, then it's the rest. Do you think Kat's coffin should be longer or not? Should they be the same or different? Wood or steel? White? Maybe white? Open or closed? I hate thinking of that caked-on make-up on my girls forever. Libi, I won't even let my girls wear makeup; they're way too young. So not too much. Those eyelids and lips sewn shut. How will they look? How will they be presented? Lulu loves Sleeping Beauty, you know, Lib. But oh my God. Which cemetery, under which tree, or on which hill? Not out by the highway. Don't you dare let Jim pick that garish place under those fast food billboards. He won't take my calls, won't speak to me. So tell him, Libi, tell him what to do. He needs that. Tell him."

"It's already decided, Terese. I don't know where they'll be, but he doesn't need anyone telling him anything. He's made the decisions."

The guard put the cuffs back on and began leading Terese away. "They keep making me talk to a counselor, Lib. It's awful. She knows nothing. She's twelve. Got her credentials online. I can't tell her anything. I hate looking at her stupid face, Lib. And telling her's my only way out." The Christmas tree changed colors, silently.

Compassion flooded into Libi's whisper. "I'll be back in a week."

"I can just see Jim stacking that wood. Making every piece the same length."

"It's perfect."

"Those pearly pens at the guest book always run out of ink, Lib. You know they do. He won't know to buy two pens. He won't think to get one for a backup. The ink is never any good. Get the good pens, Libi. Do it for him, so he doesn't have to be embarrassed. And I don't care what's been decided. You find it, you do it. Pick the best cemetery plot, make sure he doesn't rush, doesn't cop out, doesn't fuck that up. Don't you dare let him put my girls in that discount plot by the highway, I don't care what it costs for two places out there. Sell their rubies if you have to. Give them a hill, Libi. A little sloping hillside under shade trees with soft grasses and bluebells, a bird feeder, please, violets in spring. Okay? Promise. Maybe a little black bench. You have to promise. I can't take it if you don't promise. But the wood. All that wood, I can see it. See him with it, and the girls there, too, dancing in the wood chips, tossing them up. Can't you see them? With him? Kat in her pink windbreaker, Lulu in her puffy lavender boots. How he lets them play while he works. How careful he is with them. He seems so inattentive but he's not. Just when you think he's wholly neglectful he never lets them near the sharp parts of the blade, or too close to the street.

"Nothing happens in our cul-de-sac, you know that. They're perfectly safe. That's why we live there. But he still teaches them how to be alert, Libi. Makes sure they don't drift into the street where they might get hurt. They play in that arcing sawdust while he works so hard at making it right. I can see him. They absolutely are right there, with him. They can't be gone. No, Libi, they have to be there. They're his, his everything. They must have been there while he cut down the tree. They had to help him, and not get in the way. They had to, Libi. Like good little girls for Daddy. And it can't be over. Let's get rid of the tree, Lib. Don't you think? Have the girls help? They can carry the wood, stack it. They're big enough. They're gone but they'll help him with it. They're good girls, they're only ornery and disobedient with me. Not with him, never with him. And I hated him for loving them that much, that well. Didn't hate him a lot. Just—oh God, he does love splitting wood, doesn't he, Libi? He loves getting the pieces all flush in a stack. How many cords did he put there by your garage, remember? He had wood the whole length of your house. And along my back fence? Remember how the girls would climb all over it together? So sure-footed at that age. Like baby mountain goats. He gave them that fun, a new place to conquer, Lib.

"Consistent—that's what he is. With them. And I'm right, aren't I? About the wood. Quit nodding like that. I know. I know what I did. What's happened. Don't cry. Stop crying, I can't take it. It's done. It's over. He never says a word—to me, to them. He never listens to me, Lib. But he listens to them, always. And no matter what, he keeps leaving his perfection everywhere, for all of us, all three. You have to stop crying, Lib. Please stop. I can't take it. The stack of wood is what it means to be beautiful, isn't it?"

ROAST BEEF & HAVARTI

The woods had been cleared for the two men, partially. Heavy-tread machinery had flattened and raised dried mud. But on that very early morning they didn't notice what was; they were there to imagine what would be—a red-glass backsplash against slate. Surrounded by tree stumps and dew-covered construction machinery, the men, lovers, stood on the temporary plywood floor of the home they were building together. They hadn't wanted a wide green lawn flowing into the next yard. They wanted to keep the neighbors' lit windows at an arboreal distance—loved to have familial laughter close but not too close. They wanted Acadian flycatchers and a ten-minute drive into town, a place just hospitable enough, in the rolling glacial hills two and a half hours west of Cincinnati.

One man, Wyatt, was tall and thin with dark brown hair. He wore neat clothes and carefully-tied shoes. The other man, who was almost always referred to as Wyatt's boyfriend, or Wyatt's partner, or that guy who lives with Wyatt, though he did wear a required name tag at his work, was more rumpled and talked constantly about having to manage his weight. Not that morning, but on other days, usually in the evening he'd say, "I probably shouldn't eat this," and then eat, justifying consumption with a story about his terrible day. But that morning he said, "This is where the sink'll go." The man, whose mother had wanted so much to call him Henry, rarely gave up. His arms were spread in a V indicating the southeast corner. A plastic grocery bag hung from his arm.

"Why?"

"Because of the skylight."

"Skylight? Is that back in? You know it'll leak."

"We'll caulk it or whatever." He moved toward the threshold where his partner stood. While he walked he didn't look up, didn't look Wyatt in the eye, intimacy being the trouble that it is, and kept rummaging in the plastic bag. "I really don't think the overhang of the mezzanine is going to obstruct the light."

"Mezzanine?"

Impatiently he offered both sandwiches on open palms. The sun had not yet risen enough to warm the day. But it would. Spring was enlivening the underbrush. Countless tiny green leaves unfolded around them. "Yeah. You want the roast beef or the ham salad?"

Wyatt kept his distance but leaned toward the offerings. "What kind of cheese is that?"

"Havarti."

"Havarti?"

Wyatt's boyfriend, whose name (to his mother's great regret) was Len, said, "Skylight? Mezzanine? You've seen the blueprints. Now you're shocked it's Havarti? Why are you acting so stupid? You, yourself, were the one who bought the cheese. It's the only cheese we have anywhere in the fridge right now. So of course it's Havarti. What's with you?"

"It's early. I need coffee, not ham salad."

"So you want the roast beef?"

"No. What I most want is coffee. You drove right past my favorite—"

"Don't be so condescending. You said we had to decide about this today so your shit of a contractor—I still say we should have hired my uncle—will come back and finally start on the kitchen. You have to be at work by nine. I have to work until nine. So here we are. I know it's early. Get over it. Let's just make these decisions and get out of here." He pointed back emphatically to where he'd been standing. "That's where the sink should go."

To the world of good looks and good manners they were Wyatt and that other guy. But at home? Alone? Together? Wyatt loved Len, loved how the name *Leonard* had been insisted upon by Len's father's mother who felt someone should continue bearing the burden bequeathed years before to her favorite uncle. Wyatt also loved the way Len's mother never forgave her husband for not being able to stand up to his mother about the necessity of passing on such a horrific family name. Most of all Wyatt loved how Len's mom maintained passive resistance by refusing to call her child by name, instead summoning him always with *Governor-General* during those years of his most fervent passion to grow up. Wyatt never, ever used the term *Governor-General* himself, was forbidden to do so, but said as if long deputized to his station as second-in-command, "If you don't mind, I'd rather not decide this without coffee."

"Then you should have brought some coffee. You just don't want the sink over there." Len shoved the roast beef sandwich at him and moved toward the south edge of the temporary floor. He took the plastic bag off his arm and spread it on the plywood. He sat on the bag and watched his lover, who could not be forced, coaxed, or coddled in moments like this. He'd come over and sit down in his own time.

The sound of a breeze moving through the prior year's brown oak leaves was more pronounced than the noise of single cars as they sped by on the distant highway. One car would go by, then silence would return. Another would go by, then be gone again toward life.

Watching Wyatt did no good. Nothing could rush him. He was mulishly impossible. As his lover was ignoring his stare, Len lost all patience and was forced to say, "Jesus. What are you doing?"

"I'm taking the cheese off."

"Why?"

"Havarti's not a sandwich cheese."

"Yes, it is. Even if it's not, when I got to the fridge, the roast beef was all dried out 'cause you didn't close the bag. How hard is it to run two fingers along a Ziploc? Bread's dry. Beef's dry. You won't eat mayo. I had to put cheese on it to give it enough moisture so it didn't cling all up in the roof of your mouth."

"Sandwich cheeses should complement the meat, not compete with it. Swiss. Muenster. Provolone. Even American. All very good sandwich cheeses. They have mild flavors."

"What are you even talking about? Taste it. Havarti is more mild than Swiss for sure. Plus, it's cut in the damn shape of the bread. How is it not a sandwich cheese? You could have bought provolone or Muenster. You do the groceries. Why buy Havarti?"

"I didn't get the Havarti to make sandwiches! I was going to have some cheese and grapes and salami and watch a movie while you were at work one night this week. I don't like cooking a whole meal just for me."

"Have you heard of leftovers? A microwave maybe?"

"Not that it's your business, but I wanted to have a nice little cold plate."

"So this is what you do while I'm at work? You make nice little cold plates and watch old movies?"

"I don't make a habit of it. But sometimes, yes. Especially if a good movie's on. Or a bad movie that I love."

"So let me get this straight. Havarti complements salami on your cold plate, just not on the sandwich I made for you while you were preening like a guinea hen for half an hour? Are you sure you don't want to change that story?"

Wyatt had to restrain himself from addressing the Governor-General directly. "Sandwiches are different."

"Oh, professor, do tell. I so love your little lectures."

Wyatt ignored the snide tone and took him at his word. "If you're eating finger foods, one bite of cheese, then one bite of meat, the flavors linger and can blend on your palate as you alternate. But in a sandwich you get it all at once. If one flavor dominates—it just doesn't end up tasting good."

"So you need contrast on an appetizer platter, but complementary flavors in a sandwich."

"Yes."

"You and your constant bullshit! Havarti complements everything. It barely even has any flavor! You just have to be right. You are so crazy."

"I am not."

"Yes. You are."

"If I'm so crazy then you eat the roast beef and Havarti."

"You hate ham salad."

"Then don't be pissed if I take the damned Havarti off my sandwich."

They looked at the place in the dirt where a broken bag of cement had been forgotten, rained on, and turned to a mass of concrete around the base of a sugar maple they'd hoped to preserve—even tap—: the one that would shade the front sitting room. The concrete would need to be removed without killing the tree. One of them would have to call. They independently tried to remember the foreman's name.

"Don't look at me. I see it."

Wyatt never did sit down. His lover finished the ham salad sandwich and stood up again. He walked back to the best place for the sink. "What about cheddar?"

Wyatt picked up the plastic bag, which had been left behind, and put the sandwich wrap in it. But he didn't say anything to scold his lover, and he entertained the question. "Cheddar?"

"Cheddar is definitely a sandwich cheese, and it is certainly not always mild."

"Cheddar's different."

Len didn't want to be bothered. He threw crust out toward the cement around the tree. "How?"

"I don't know. I don't like it."

"Neither do I. Except with apples. In the fall."

Wyatt conceded. "Or on Ritz crackers—you know those crocks of spread your sister sends from Wisconsin every October after we go apple-picking?"

"With the little round knife. So good. I love those little wooden-handled spreaders."

Wyatt eased his previous restraint, took quite a severe tone with his lover. "We're not moving all fourteen of those spreaders to this new kitchen. I am not going to look at your drawers of clutter in a brand new house."

"Half of them have fallen apart because you let them soak."

"You let the cheese dry on the blade." Then, thinking of apple-picking with their nieces, Wyatt redirected them both. Or tried. "I love cheddar. Just not on sandwiches."

"You and your cold plates. Is that why you're always drunk when I get home late?"

"Wine goes well with cheese and meat."

Len mimicked him. "Wine goes well with cheese and meat. Can you be more droll?"

"Why are you attacking me? Would you look at that sunrise and just relax? We both have a long day today. Look around you. Those uprights are the beginnings of our home together. Our home. No one else's. Let's figure out this sink placement."

"Ours and no one else's, until you sell it."

"Why would I sell it?"

Len threw up both hands in mock defeat. "You were already talking about the property values going up and all that."

"Why wouldn't you want the property values to go up?"

"It doesn't matter if you're not going to sell it."

"But increasing property values is just an indicator of how nice a place is to live."

"So why don't you say, *I hope we have a nice place to live that gets even nicer?*"

Wyatt traced his eyebrow with one finger. "Nice place? Gets even nicer? I may be droll, but at least I'm an adult."

"You are the farthest thing from an adult. Cold plates are like damn kindergarten snack time." Len had planted himself where the sink should be. But his lover seemed to be ignoring the issue, wandering around picking up trash, putting it into the plastic bag. The Governor-General was not kind at all and almost shouted, "Please! Just answer me! Where do you want the sink?"

"I told you where I want the sink."

"When?"

"Wherever you want it."

"Wyatt. What? When did you say that?"

"I don't have to say that. That's what's going to end up happening or I'll hear about it every day for the next fifteen years, until I sell our home in a selfish fit of greed related to the increased property values."

Len ignored the sarcasm, focused on the sink placement. "And you're sure?"

"Yes."

"Fine. Then that's where it'll go."

Almost disappointed that he'd won, Len said, "Why are you being so conciliatory all of a sudden?"

"It's your sink."

"I'm not doing all the dishes."

Wyatt stopped and faced this man, lowered his voice, disengaging completely from their comfortable years of interminable bickering banter. "I know. But you're the morning person. And standing there, where you want your sink to go, with the roseate light falling all around you, is perfect. If you were stunning, it'd be stunning. So yes, you can have your skylight. And yes, you can put your sink in that corner. Because as many days as possible I want to walk into this kitchen in the mornings and see you in that light. It's our morning light, and this is our home."

"Really?"

"Really."

ROGUES

Kris was groggy every homogenous morning that
summer after seventh grade. Not wanting to wake
parents, she dug through the freezer for ice as quietly as
she could, letting water from the faucet slowly fill the
insulated jug of ice cubes. Her step-mom had left her two
bologna sandwiches, a stick of string cheese, and a
twenty-ounce bottle of pop, precious and rare in a house
full of older brothers. She also grabbed a package of
Cheetos and the portioned bags of grapes and blueberries
she had left in the freezer overnight. All of it went into
the cooler that she pulled down off the fridge. By the

time her lunch was packed, the jug of water was overflowing. She turned off the faucet.

In the mudroom she pawed through the pile of laundry on top of the drier and pulled out a faded blue sweatshirt, her favorite, the one with all the names from her brother's 1986 varsity squad screen-printed in two red rows on the back. She put on her filthy tennis shoes. Dust found its way between her already too-hot toes. She grabbed her work gloves and was careful not to let the screen door slam.

The sky was nearly through with its work of pushing away the night as she moved her ten-speed bike, an old pink hand-me-down Huffy, out of the detached garage. She put the lunch cooler on one of the handle bars and her jug of water on the other, and took off, standing up on the pedals to get the old thing moving.

It was about a ten minute ride to the courthouse. A few other kids were there when she arrived—sitting on the peaked cement coping, eating donuts from the bakery. Two of the boys were roughhousing, but most of the kids were immobile and quiet. She didn't bother to acknowledge anyone and no one acknowledged her. It was early and they had the rest of the day to talk. She locked her bike with the others and set down her lunch cooler on the dewy courthouse lawn near two of her friends.

"Want anything?" She tilted her head towards the bakery.

One friend—well, not exactly a friend—a girl named Regina, shook her head and fell backwards on the lawn, yawning, covering her face with her arm. Their friend Melanie held up her half-eaten nut roll, indicating she'd already gotten what she needed. Kris stared down at the street, listening, not looking for cars, and walked into the old bakery with its pressed-tin ceiling. Weather-beaten farmers sat silent with their steaming coffee. Kris bought an apple fritter and a large Styrofoam cup of milk. A customer opened the white-frame screen door and Kris went back to the coping across the street. She sat down between Melanie and Regina. Melanie reached for the milk and took a sip without comment. Regina kept her arm over her face and feigned sleep.

Kris tried not to pay attention, but there he was in the intersection, their foreman, Kyle.

He was a sophomore in high school, sixteen. She was only going into eighth grade. She knew what that meant, what it should mean. Moving with a slow intention, he peeled a hard-boiled egg, threw pieces of shell in the street.

He didn't really look for her, either, probably wouldn't. She stared at the bakery and let him approach, kept him visible in her peripheral vision. Didn't let on she was interested. He didn't come very close, wouldn't.

That's how they had been since May—aware of each other but avoidant. But Kris's neck surged hot if he talked to the girl with the green shoes. And Kyle, well, Kyle seemed to get more agitated if Kris reacted too much to the kid who'd always come up behind her to snap her bra. Kyle didn't like that kid at all. But he never said a word to Kris, or to that bratty kid, or to anyone else. He'd just monitor from a distance.

It was impossible to tell if he cared. His agitation could have been related to a general sense of what was right in a situation and not necessarily to her.

As the kids assembled, more and more bikes were locked up at the racks, and more and more noise was made: the clattering of plastic coolers against the concrete coping, soles of shoes scraping against the courthouse's sidewalk steps, boys' laughter and commentary as they pushed, shoved, and jumped over each other from lawn to sidewalk, shoving each other into all the imagined dangers of the vacant street. As she lay across the grass that one boy stepped on Regina's ponytail, hoping she would sit up and pull her hair. But she ignored him, lay still, and he went away to fall dramatically over the curb as if it were a real barrier to his climb.

Right at 5:30 a.m., an old tan school bus pulled up to the courthouse. On its side were painted the company name and logo, and underneath, a line of script carefully articulated in green paint: "Hybridizing Seed Corn since 1973." Without any notice of the company's history, the kids got up, gathered their sweatshirts and lunch coolers, and converged at the bus door. The boys pushed each other out of line and ran around the girls, swooping in and out like barn swallows.

Picking seats was a quiet quick affair. Kris wanted to be with Kyle but Regina sat down next to her instead. He stayed near the front, talked to the driver. She watched him, longing for a different arrangement and then gave up.

The bus began moving, rattling and shifting through gears. Small towns seem bigger early in the morning, Kris thought. She looked out the window as they passed the ice cream stand by the river, passed the statue of General Milroy in his triangular park, passed the judge's house, the Pizza King, the elementary school, the grocery store, the Catholic college. Finally they got into fifth gear on the stem-straight country highway connecting the town to the interstate.

After the bus had bounced along between freshly painted yellow and white lines for twenty minutes, it turned in that pivoting way, with a slightly precarious lean. The new road was unmarked, paved only for the first mile. Then its surface switched to gravel. The bus, with some windows always stuck down, soon filled with a cloud of limestone dust. The kids barely noticed.

In May, they were paid to pick up rocks. In June, they were paid to rogue. In July, they would detassel, and by August there would be no more work to do. They would be back in school and quiet field winds would work on, carrying pollen to the female rows. When the silks were purple and deepening, the male rows would be cut down. It would be Fall. November winds would dry the female cornstalks to rustling readiness, loosened. Once harvested, the seed would be moved in red trucks to the drying elevator, and the female rows would be plowed under, just like the males had been months before. Hybridizing seed corn was important work. The male rows had certain attributes that would be good for the next year's corn. So did the female ones. But male or female, any strange stalks couldn't be allowed to reproduce. The next year's corn had to fit the machinery if the yields were to be high—uniformity helped. The girls knew it. And they were just the same. They knew that, too.

Arriving at the edge of a field, the bus slowed and eased off the road by a ditch. Mr. Allen, their supervisor, who wore the same old ball cap every day, sat there in his company pickup, waiting for them. As the bus stopped he got out of his truck, spat, grabbed a clipboard, and stooped, pulled himself shoulders first into the bus.

"Listen up. We're going to rogue the Elijah fields this morning, and then walk beans after lunch. It's supposed to storm later on. So we're going to walk these fields twice, not three times, this morning. We'll double back next week. Lunch will be pushed up so we can get over to those beans as early as possible. So today's a hustle."

The kids stood and began moving forward, leaving coolers and water jugs shaded under their bus seats.

They froze when his voice rang out again. "Wait. One point of business. I need to see Thompson." Mr. Allen looked down at his clipboard. "Jason Thompson. It's about your W-2."

In order to be well off the thin gravel road, the driver had parked the bus so that it leaned out over the deep ditch. But the kids just adapted. They jumped deep down into the ditch and crawled up the other side, scrambling, pulling at tall weeds to help their ascent. They followed each other—not reluctant, but not in a hurry—to the bed of the pickup and each grabbed a wooden-handled shovel.

The shovel blades were cut straight across and filed sharp. The kids pulled black trash bags out of a huge cardboard box and began biting them at the seams, creating holes for their heads and arms. Then, dressed in the black trash bags, they splayed out along the rows of growing corn.

There was no giddy chatter yet. Kris, Regina, and Melanie moved silently through the scraggly border of the cool early morning dew-covered field. Kris pulled on her mud-caked gloves. Melanie craned her neck every few steps, looking back toward Jason, who was still talking to Mr. Allen.

Regina said, "Kris, why don't you just tell him?"

"Tell who what?"

"Tell Kyle you like him."

"Why?"

"Because it's weird how you hover around, looking sideways all the time."

"I don't look sideways."

"Melanie, doesn't she do that?"

"Regina, can't you ever mind your own business?"

"I don't see why you're even interested in that guy. He's so scrawny. It's like his stomach is all sunken in and makes his back arch at the top or something, with his shoulders all—I don't know."

Kris said nothing.

Regina went on, "But whatever. It's not like any of us are going to fight you for him. Just say something."

Kris didn't respond. She looked up to where Kyle was walking ahead of them, hoped he couldn't hear. Regina was so loud all the time.

"Or. Fine. Don't. See if I care. But. Don't be surprised if he gets another girlfriend, and don't come crying to me about it, all sad and mopey."

Melanie defended Kris, "Shut up, Regina. No one wants to hear you right now."

The girls fell into the lineup—a kid to every male row of corn. Regina, Kris, and Melanie took their positions at the end of a row. "Hey! Scoot down one. Jason's coming."

Kris's hair loosened in its ponytail. It never mattered how tightly she pulled it—it always came loose. She pushed a strand behind her ear, staked her shovel three inches into the uneven loam, and put her foot up on the side. She waited, ready, wearing the trash bag and leaning her chin on her arm. She steadied the handle of her shovel.

The rising sun had conquered the distant treetops.

Melanie watched Jason hand the clipboard back to Mr. Allen. She had already gotten him a trash bag and a shovel, and she motioned for him to join her and her friends. His buddies hollered at him from down the line, but he waved them off and jogged towards Melanie. She handed him the trash bag first. He was more fastidious about tailoring his makeshift slicker, didn't just bite and tear at the plastic. For him it was important to remain civilized as he carefully tore a v-shape from the center of the bag's base and a half-circle on each side. They all respected him. But like the others he pulled the bag over his head, adjusted it as best he could, clung to what pride remained, and then took the shovel from Melanie.

As soon as he was ready, Mr. Allen shouted, "Okay. Down and back."

The kids moved into the corn.

The instructions were to cut down any plant that was at all different from the others: if a stalk was too thick, cut it down, if it was too dark a green, cut it down, too insipid-looking or yellow, cut it, too tall, slice right through. In June the plants were surging with their chance to grow.

Kris walked to the left of the male row. The ground was still wet under a thin layer of dried topsoil so her feet sank with each step. The furrows made her footing unsure. She walked carefully and watched for clods of dirt and unexpected dips. The corn was about four feet tall and laden with morning dew. Leaves unloaded the water caught under millions of hair-holds onto the plastic she wore. The trash bag kept only her sweatshirt dry. Water soaked her old jean shorts. After they were saturated, the water began to run down, and her sneakers filled with water. She was chilled. The weight and girth of the mud made her footing even more unsteady, but she was used to these mornings in the fields.

She scanned her rows. There. She plunged the shovel down quickly, slicing through the cornstalk she had singled out. She did not stop but always worked in motion, walking up the row, inspecting her territory, slicing down aberrant plants.

A rogue was anything out of the ordinary.

The row of kids moved steadily through the field, all alerted to variation. They began to wake up to the rustle of trash bags and leaves, to the sounds of intermittent slicing, to the movement of cool wind drying the acres.

As she worked, Kris imagined a life with Kyle, and also one without him. They were pretty much the same. She'd still be herself. But she did watch him, Regina was right about that. He was more thoughtful with her than he was with anyone else, though it wasn't totally clear if he'd really given her any kind of special treatment. He was pretty nice to everyone, polite, courteous. She couldn't tell if she just liked that about him or if there were something kind of important between them, something theirs. They were almost like two hesitant, searching rain drops that rove slow and searchingly across a windshield, quivering, resistant even when totally impeded by a speck of debris. Never did the raindrops stop there though. Almost always they finally seemed to find each other, join, and rush on with something so like the joy of having found someone.

Kyle wasn't from any kind of rich family, if that stuff mattered. Once he had talked about helping his mom put plastic over the windows, had made them all laugh with a story about his standing outside his little sister's bedroom window with an orange extension cord and a hair dryer. How his little sister woke up from her nap screaming because she had no idea what he was doing.

But Kris got it. There had been several years of her childhood over at her dad's when they didn't even have a door on the front of the house. They'd boarded it up with plywood and asked everyone to come in through the garage. It had been a big deal when Kris's dad went to the industrial wholesale place and got a new storm door for their family, had come with two of his high school buddies, torn out the old plywood and mildewed wall board, rebuilt the frame, and hung that door. Kris's step-mom had been kind of ashamed but very, very grateful. Her dad didn't say much about it. Maybe Kyle would be like that. Do something nice like that.

What if he didn't, though? What if he showed up with a bunch of friends at her mom's and took all the baby ducks out of their pond? That borrow pit pond was Kris's mom's pride and joy. She'd built a little island in it, with a shingled wishing well and a bucket that dropped down. What if Kyle came with his friends, waded out there, and tipped it over? It wasn't worth it. High school boys were always doing stupid things. Kris's big brothers were evidence of that. Or what if he didn't understand about the miscarriages Kris's mom had had after the boys were born, why there were so many years before Kris came along? What if he said something dumb about the age gap? Or about her step-dad's fishing trophy, the one his buddy gave him before he died, the one Kris's middle brother painted purple when he was thirteen? It looked bizarre on the shelf in the basement but it was special, important, and Kyle might not know not to say anything about it.

Plus Kyle didn't actually have a car yet. So how would he even get out to her mom's place? It was nine miles out in the country. She had to take the bus home on the days she stayed with her mom and step-dad. The high school wasn't close to the middle school. And there was no damn way Kris's step-dad would let Kyle come over to her dad's place in town.

There wasn't really a point to tell Kyle anything. Regina was such a pain in the ass. She should have just left well enough alone. But Kris knew she'd say something. So now Kris would have to tell him for no reason, with no real prospect of doing anything together. Why should she?

She didn't want to.

Regina shouted over to Jason. "What'd he say about your W-2?"

Melanie said, "God, Regina. Seriously. Stay out of everybody else's business, would you?"

Regina switched her focus back to matchmaking. "If Krissy doesn't want to tell him, she doesn't have to. But she should. Look at her. She hasn't taken her eyes off that sickly-looking guy since we started. Is she ever going to look him in the eye? No. Is she ever even going to smile or say anything nice to him? No. You know how she is."

"I'm right here. Can you please stop talking about me?"

"You know you won't."

"Why do you care so much what I do?"

"Because you're going to end up in some dead-end dental hygienist's job or something and no one's even going to care."

"Dental hygienist? What are you even talking about?"

Melanie added. "Yeah. How is that even a dead-end job? My cousin Missy does that. It's great money. She never has to work any nights or holidays. She loves it."

Kris said, "I'm not going to be a dental hygienist, Regina. And I won't call you crying if Kyle gets a different girlfriend."

"Yes you will."

"No. I won't." The finality shut Regina up momentarily. In the East, the sun had finally risen enough to blind any fixed stare. The line of workers moved steadily forward but it also undulated. Each kid moved at roughly the same pace as those around him or her, but the row expanded and contracted and bulged out in places as Kris looked over at everyone in the line. The morning's cool dewy haze was gone.

"Krissy! Hey. To your right, not your left. Pay attention!"

Kris looked back over her shoulder. Kyle, beyond content in his role as the foreman, sliced an obviously too-thick stalk out of one of her female rows. "Sorry, Kyle. Thanks." She watched him move back and forth across the rows of seven of the kids. He was a little taller and could see the rogues from further away. But he had that way of half judging her. It was so, *something*. It was as though he held her to a higher standard for some reason, expected more.

Regina shouted to Kyle, who was working his way back to the East. "Kyle, Krissy just wants you to follow right behind her. That's why she missed that obvious one."

Melanie turned to Regina. "Shut up, Regina."

Regina turned. "Come on, Krissy, he'll catch up. You don't have to wait for Kyle back there."

Jason joined his girlfriend in defense of Kris. "Regina, don't be like that."

Regina retorted. "Melanie, tell your stupid boyfriend to shut up."

None of the kids talked to each other for a while, concentrating on their rows.

Most fields were a mile long. But the Elijah fields were longer. The motion through the fields was slow, but eventually they reached the other side. When Kris, Regina, Jason, and Melanie came to the end of their rows, some other kids were already finished and were sitting on their shovels or using the shovel blades to scrape mud from their shoes.

Kris turned to Melanie. "He's a lot older. My mom won't like it. I don't even think my dad will let him in the house."

Melanie nodded, "Or let you out of it."

When all the kids and all the foremen were out of the rows, and Mr. Allen had walked back and forth counting the kids twice, he signaled with an arm over his head and all the kids turned around and moved into the rows again.

Back down the same rows.

Stepping over rocks and this time over cut-down rogues too.

There was just as much work to do walking back as there had been walking down. There were always more aberrations—the stalks seen from a different perspective, the ones overlooked the first time in attending to the destruction of others.

Kris planted her feet in the soil, steadying herself. She said to Regina, "Will it make you happy if I do say something to Kyle?"

Regina laughed. "Not really. But it might make you happy. And probably him, too." She pointed at him with her shovel.

Kris was embarrassed. It was like Regina wanted Kyle to hear the whole thing, wouldn't just shut up and be discreet about anything. "How do you know if it'd make him happy?"

"You're so dense."

"Really? You think so?"

"That you're dense? No. That he likes you? Yes."

"Are you sure?"

"No. And neither are you. Just tell him."

Back on the original side of the field the day was fully bright and hot. The dew had dried and the trash bags were humid inside and dry on the outside. The kids peeled the bags off themselves and piled them in the back of Mr. Allen's pickup. Kris took off her sweatshirt and tied it around her waist. Down the rows and back again, then a water break. Someone had seen a pheasant. Someone else had fallen and hit his knee on a piece of drainage tile. The kids watched Mr. Allen pouring peroxide over the scrape and listened to the kid tell how it hurt worse than the time he flipped a four-wheeler.

Kris edged away from the group and sipped water that was too cold on her teeth. Kyle looked over at her, caught her glance for a second, smiled. She looked away involuntarily. It was just instinct. Had he smiled? She tried to recover, to look again, but he'd turned his back and was walking up toward another of the foremen, to have some discussion. Kris felt divided from everything. Cheap paper cups arched through the air into the bed of the truck as the workers finished up their break. She turned back around and Regina was right there making a silent kissy face at her. Kris ignored her, mouthing back, "You're so immature."

One nod from Mr. Allen dispersed the kids back toward the rows with their sharpened shovels. They had to wait to be counted again. Kris looked at the blisters on her palms. In another week they'd be calluses.

Regina walked up to Kris, poked her on a sunburned shoulder and said, "You're the one who's immature. Just tell him."

Kris hissed, "I will."

"When? When you're ready? And when will that be?" Regina raised her shovel and slammed it into a big dirt clod, which crumbled. "If you don't tell him, I will, Krissy."

"Don't you dare. It has nothing to do with you."

"Right now it has nothing to do with you either and it's your life."

Melanie said to Kris, "You know she'll do it." And then to Regina, "Leave her alone. What's with you? Why do you care?"

"I don't. I'm just sick of her sulking around all crushing on him."

"It really doesn't concern you."

"How does it not? Every time I try to talk to her, she's staring over my shoulder watching him. I'm sick of it. They need to just get together or get over it."

"Fine. I'll tell him today."

"Oh, you will not, and you know it."

"I absolutely will."

"Well, good. I'll be glad when you do." Regina leaned on Kris. "Plus, Krissy, just think, if you tell him and he likes you too, Kyle will bring you gifts just like Jason brings Melanie. Remember how he brought her that pretty dolphin necklace from Myrtle Beach?" Regina tried not to laugh. Both Kris and Regina thought the necklace was ugly. The girls knew Melanie thought it was ugly too, but she would never admit it. She wore it every day.

Kris knew Regina was jealous of Melanie, who had long curly auburn hair and a real boyfriend. Regina's hair was thin and straight and always went limp even if she tried to curl it. Kris turned away from Regina's stare so that Melanie and Jason wouldn't perceive any commiseration.

Jason spoke to Melanie for a moment confidentially and then moved ahead to rejoin his buddies. As soon as he was out of earshot Regina said, "Why do you even wear that necklace, Melly? It's atrocious."

Melanie turned to Regina. "Because he was thinking of me when we were apart."

Regina chewed her thumbnail. "He must not have been thinking very hard."

Kris intervened. "Shut up, Regina. I don't see your loser boyfriend bringing you any jewelry from anywhere."

Regina was going with an older boy who was contracting that summer. He was responsible for fifteen fields of corn and had five other high school guys working with him. "That's because he doesn't go anywhere. He's always working. He's only got five guys in his crew this summer and they've got a ton of acres. He's making lots of money. He's saving up."

"To do what? Go drinking with his buddies at that stupid abandoned gas station? When has he ever taken you anywhere since he got his license?" Melanie raised her voice. The day was getting hot. "Kris doesn't have to say anything if she doesn't want to. The boy's supposed to say something to her. Not everyone's as slutty as you are, Regina."

"How am I slutty?"

"How are you not?"

The girls moved into the field when Mr. Allen finally motioned for them to start.

Regina shouted after they had worked for almost thirty yards. "I'm slutty because he took me to the movies?"

Melanie laughed. "Movies? What? That day does not count. His mom sent you to babysit his little sister, because she knew she couldn't trust her own son when she had to work. You guys saw a cartoon."

"Well, we made out even if it was a cartoon."

Kris said, "You made out in front of his little sister? That's trashy, Regina. I didn't say you were slutty, but that's what Melly's talking about."

"His little sister fell asleep in the air conditioning. It was fine."

"It's gross."

The girls lifted up their shovels and brought them down hard through the rogues—killing them off.

Cumulus clouds formed on the horizon. The corn leaves began to curl up. The foremen shouted to each other and then to their crews to work a little faster.

Regina stopped and pointed across the rows to a stalk in Kris's purview. "Quit daydreaming, Krissy. You missed one."

"Which one?"

"That one right there."

"What are you talking about? That one's fine."

"No it's not. Look at the color."

"The color is fine."

"That shrively part."

"What are you talking about?" Kris's frustration grew. The kids all stopped, craned their necks, stared at the one stalk Regina had implicated.

Regina would not be silenced. "Kris. You need to do your job."

Kris snapped back. "You need to shut your mouth."

"Shut my what?"

"Your big mouth. Always telling everybody what to do, how to do it. What about that one, there, in your row? Why don't you worry about that?"

"I haven't gotten there yet."

"It's right there. You can reach it from where you're standing. You would have walked right past it worrying about what I'm doing. Telling me to cut down perfectly good plants."

"It's not good. Look at it from over here. From this side."

"If there's something wrong with it from that side, I'll see it on the way back. Why don't you just drop it? There's nothing wrong with it at all. From this side. Which. Is where I am."

"Why so defensive? I was just trying to help you out." Regina paused, looked around, saw that all their friends were watching, seemed to need someone in a position of authority to corroborate her opinion. "Kyle!"

Kyle looked up, looked at Kris first instinctively, then at Regina who had demanded his attention.

Regina shouted again, "Come look at this stalk. Kris wants to save it. It's all shrively. Probably full of aphids."

Kris was rarely drawn into arguments but it was the heat of the day. "There are no aphids, Kyle. You don't need to come over here."

But Kyle was already near her, looking at the stalk.

Regina must have seen some acceptance of the thing in his face. She insisted, "This side. Look."

Kyle was not one to be bossed around by a thirteen-year-old girl, especially not by Regina. He did not budge.

Regina changed her tactics. "Please. You have to see it from over here."

Kyle looked at Kris. Their eyes locked for a moment, and then he looked away, but seemed to consent. He used two hands to push the corn aside, stepped through the rows, slow in the heat, slow enough not to damage the plants.

He didn't stand as close to Regina as he had stood next to Kris. But he saw what Regina meant, must have. He came back to Kris, reached out his hand.

Kris refused.

"You want to look at it, or not?"

Kris's voice was quiet, controlled. "I am looking at it."

"No, you're not. You're looking at me."

"And?"

His tenderness ebbed. He likely didn't want to be exposed in front of the others. "Kris. Give me the shovel."

"No. This is my row. That plant is fine."

He leaned toward her, all the warmth of his heart seeming to return, less ashamed, less frightened. He said without touching her hair, without reaching out to her at all, "Just cut it down. How many plants are there? Thousands. This one will not make a difference."

She wouldn't give him her shovel. "It makes a difference to me," she whispered, hoping he'd come back into the moment they'd shared just before.

He wouldn't. He seemed compelled to broadcast his callousness. His arm shot out in her direction. "Hand it over."

Kris absolutely would not give him her shovel, not right then.

He nodded, but turned to Regina, who thrust her shovel right over. Kyle didn't hesitate. He sliced through the stalk with one perfected gesture.

It was too much for Krissy.

He handed the borrowed shovel back and kept walking.

Regina's voice was full of fury. "Kris. What's wrong with you? Why are you crying over this? It is not that big of a deal."

Kris couldn't take it. "Sometimes I hate you, Regina."

"You hate me because of a corn plant? That's real mature, Kris. Some friend you are."

Kris's pride returned, in full force. She squinted and sniffed, getting the tears to submit. "No. Not because of a corn plant. I hate you because you can never let anyone else be right. And you were not right, Regina. There was nothing wrong with that plant. You know it. You just won't admit anything, have to have your way."

Regina turned back to her work, slammed her shovel hard through the stalk that Kris had pointed out. "Happy?"

"Like it matters."

Kyle didn't comfort Kris as he passed by, not quite; he did reach out and touch her forearm with one knowing finger. He pressed that finger softly into her flesh the way he might have pressed it into the quivering warmth of a sniffling guinea pig. As quietly, he pulled his finger away with the same boyish uncertainty about how best to treat such a strange new-found thing. He got ten feet away and was all manhood again when he shouted, "Let's go, you guys. Come on."

Melanie hurried from behind, leaving Jason to find his friends. "Wait up, girls!"

Each foreman lingered until his seven kids were out of the field, counted them and then sent them right back up the rows as Mr. Allen had instructed. Every kid worked hard, scanning the rows, cutting down rogues, and walking fast. The corn leaves, dry now, sliced their shins, thighs, and arms and left dozens of tiny cuts, like paper cuts, on their skin. Kyle moved behind Kris's group, encouraging them to keep up the pace so they could get back to the bus for lunch.

Kris didn't particularly want to do what he wanted right then. She fell back, resistant. But he seemed to understand in the way he came and walked near her, two rows over. He didn't rush her; she stopped lagging. Neither said a word.

In the bus, the girls found their way to their seats. Jason sat down next to Melanie and put his arm around her. She turned her head and spoke to him. No one else heard the conversation. Kris drank from her jug of water, still cold from all the morning's ice cubes. Regina let her ponytail drape over the back of the seat so that it was in the lap of the boy behind her.

"Get your nasty hair off me, Regina."

"Shut up. I'm just trying to rest for a minute."

"Well, put your hair on your side of the seat."

"Fine. Whatever." Regina tossed her head and after brushing her hair across his lap several times, pulled her ponytail back onto her side of the seat.

The bus took them to a farmhouse near the fields they would work in the afternoon. The driver parked in the shade of some sycamore trees by a pole barn and the kids unloaded themselves with their lunch coolers. They spread out over the front lawn, and sat down to eat. There was a row of portable toilets near the lawn, which was perfectly maintained. Geraniums grew in a prim plastic goose on an Astroturf side porch.

Melanie, Kris, Regina, and Jason sat in the shade of a sycamore. Jason started on a smashed peanut butter and jelly sandwich. Regina ate a packaged cupcake. Melanie opened a tiny Tupperware container filled with potato salad.

Kris hadn't quite forgiven Kyle or Regina. She pulled a wet washcloth out of a Baggie of witch hazel and wiped her face and then her hands with it. It cooled her off. Without actually wanting to, she handed it to Regina whose hand was out. "You think of everything, Krissy. That's why I love you." Regina passed the washcloth to Melanie who ran it over the back of her neck and then Jason's neck.

Kris pulled out her still frozen blueberries and grapes. She sucked on a slushy grape and pressed it against the roof of her mouth. "Then should I hate you because you think of nothing?" Regina handed the washcloth back and stuck out her tongue. "Well it's a better reason than over a stupid cornstalk." Mockery kept them both at bay. Kris finally smiled and dropped it. "I don't hate you."

Kyle came over and sprawled near them. He wasn't quite himself, though. His relaxed attractiveness had turned into something shy, then confident, then restless, then self-conscious, then jittery. "It's supposed to rain. Mr. Allen needs us to walk those drill beans. If the field really gets wet tonight we won't be able to get into it for another two weeks. All that pigweed and mustard will have taken hold by then. Rain or no rain, we're not going home until at least three, unless you hear thunder. And then maybe even if you do."

Regina looked at him. "Are you serious? He can't do that."

"We're not rogueing this afternoon. No shovels to attract the lightning. And he won't keep us out there if it's really pouring. But if it's just sprinkling he wants to get that field done."

Kris listened to him and laid the folded washcloth carefully on her thigh, near enough that he could grab it if he wanted. Kyle picked it up and rubbed it between his hands and around his fingers. He folded it exactly the way she had folded it and put it back on her thigh exactly where he had picked it up. She was smiling involuntarily. He pretended not to notice, then winked a quick wink at her.

Kris looked at him but kept eating her lunch. She listened to everything he said and started on her string cheese. She wanted to say something but didn't know how. "You want my Cheetos?"

"You're not gonna eat them?"

"I always bring too much." She handed him the bag.

"Thanks." He rolled over and lay on his back, looking up into the sycamore tree. Then he shifted and propped his head on her outstretched ankle.

Kris suppressed her reaction—the glee of contact, the desire to yank her foot away to let his head drop. She pulled a blade of grass and ran it through her fingertips.

It seemed Regina had been brooding since Melanie had confronted her. She said, "Kyle. What do those guys do at that old gas station anyway?"

Kyle laughed. "Not much. Drink beer. Light fireworks. Shoot road signs. Stupid shit."

Regina ran her fingers through Melanie's hair. "But like who goes up there? Is it just guys?"

"Mostly. You checking up on your little boyfriend, Regina? Why don't you ask him what he does? Don't ask me to watch him for you."

"I'm not. He calls me every night. He tells me everything. I just wondered if girls go too." Regina started to braid Melanie's hair.

"Once in a while. But I better never catch you up there. You're way too young."

"I'm only three years younger than you, Kyle."

"Thirteen's still a whole lot different than being sixteen."

Melanie said, "Gina's boyfriend just turned seventeen. He thinks he's hot because he got his license and he goes over there now. She's just worried about that other girl from Tri-County."

"No. I've never seen him with a girl up there. He's younger than most of the guys so he just stands around looking stupid, sipping on the one or two beers they give him. Nothin' crazy."

Jason, who would be turning fifteen at the end of September, said, "My dad's already looking around for a truck for me. I'm saving money this summer and next summer. Then we're going to split the price when I turn sixteen."

Kyle sat all the way up. "What are you looking for?"

"Black. Something small. S-10 maybe."

"What year?"

"Doesn't matter as long as it runs."

"That shouldn't set you back too much."

Regina dropped Melanie's braid, irritated by the guys talking to each other. "Kyle, why don't you ask Mr. Allen how much longer we have?"

"You already know. We've got like five minutes."

Kris got up and headed for the portable toilets. Melanie followed and Regina did too, after saying, "Whatever, Kyle. I'll ask him myself."

Mr. Allen had been inside the farmhouse eating his lunch with his friends in their air conditioned kitchen. But right then he came out on the side-porch holding a glass of lemonade. "Five minutes," he said. "Put your coolers on the bus. Get some water. Then line up from the driveway here, to as far down the road as you can. I want each of you to stand five paces apart. That means when you get to the last person on the row, you stop and count five steps with your left foot, and then stop. Then the next person counts their five paces off you. You'll be spread out enough that we can cover this whole field in one shot—down and back. Pull everything growing that's not soybeans. Let's get to it." Mr. Allen turned to take his empty glass back inside the house. In another minute he was outside again with his clipboard, wearing his hat.

Kris returned to the sycamore shade from the portable toilets and looked for her cooler. Kyle shouted to her from inside the bus. "Krissy. Don't worry. I got it. I put it here on your seat."

She went over to the bus. "Thanks, Kyle. Can you put this over there too?" She handed him her sweatshirt through the half-open window and smiled.

Kyle held the sweatshirt. "Anything for you, little Krissy."

"Little? No more Cheetos for you." He didn't say anything back: just waited there so near her, more patient with her than she felt comfortable about.

Regina came up behind her. "Let's go, Kris. Kyle just needs to get over himself. And since you're not going to do what you said you'd do, you need to get over him too."

Regina mouthed, "I'm telling him, Kris. I will tell him. So you'd better."

Kris couldn't take it. She hated how Regina insisted on things. The three girls, soon-to-be tan with sun-bleached arm hair, walked up the gravel road. Cornfields, soybean fields, the work was the same and different every day. It was the same and it was different every season, every year. The workers were the same and the workers were different over time. Kris was first to the end of the line. She counted five paces and stopped. Regina moved on, counting five paces in a singsong voice, and stopped. And Melanie went on carefully counting three paces and then backing up to Regina to start over and count five better paces so she would definitely come out right.

The girls waited for the signal and then walked into the field. Bushy soybean leaves swirled around their thighs. Kyle came up behind the girls, imitating Mr. Allen in a booming voice. "Drill beans aren't planted in rows but in swirls; the seeds are drilled into the soil. This kind of planting increases the yield per acre and minimizes the area available for weeds. But weeds still abound."

Kyle pushed Regina's shoulder almost hard enough to tip her over.

"Quit it, Kyle."

Kris steeled herself, ready for Regina to blurt it out to him, ashamed already as though it had happened. She tried to get Regina to look at her, waved her arms, but Regina's back was to her; so was Kyle's.

Why did Regina have to say anything? Why did
she want to tell him? What was the point? Kris's parents
weren't going to let him take her anywhere for at least a
year. The best she could hope was that maybe her step-
dad would hire him to help out around their place. Maybe
put up some hay or mend the fencing. But what was the
point of that? That wouldn't be a boyfriend. That'd just
be another hired hand for her step-dad.

Kris was glad when Kyle moved away from the
girls and began working with Jason and his buddies.

The girls wore their gloves and pulled out those
tall prairie weeds all the way through the field. The clouds
moved across the sky and shaded the girls from the sun
as they laughed, shouted, and bickered, while flirting with
boys. They worked hard.

Kris wanted the day to be over, wanted to be
home already, to have an ice cream sandwich on the back
deck after her shower.

But maybe Kyle could borrow his mom's car, or
come home with one of Kris's brothers. They were
always going back and forth in and out of town.

Within the hour the rain started. Mr. Allen, having
planned well, had them out of the field and already lined

up for the bus, expeditiously, safely, with almost all the work done.

The steps and the aisle of the bus were caked with several seasons of mud. Weeks and months of their toil had dried into a layer about three inches thick in the aisle and made getting to a seat difficult. Regina ended up in the back of the bus with two other girls and six of the boys, looking at a toad that one kid had found in the soybean field. Since Regina had gone to the back of the bus, Kyle sat down next to Kris. Kris knew Regina had removed herself on purpose, to be nice, in her obnoxious, controlling way of being nice, leaving her seat open for him.

Melanie and Jason leaned on each other and looked out the bus windows at the rain. Kris didn't know how to do that—how to be two people together in everything like that. She wasn't sure it was even something she wanted. Except—then Regina was back, flouncing down in the seat in front of them, blathering (mostly to them, somewhat to the girl across the aisle) about how the toad—it was an ugly, stupid little American toad—had hopped out of one kid's hand, how it had gotten on her, how another boy had grabbed it too high up on her leg, but how she'd been glad when he threw it out the window, though she hoped the little thing had made it all the way to the ditch, to some standing water, because it would be terrible if it just dropped down onto the road and got them killed. All it had really done was hop onto her leg. That's no reason for anything to have to die.

Kris and Kyle weren't listening. Kris was finally close enough to him to know it would be all right. Regina was right, she should tell him, tell him he sort of seemed to matter.

Big raindrops fell on the roof of the bus. She scooted to her right just enough so that their shoulders, arms, and legs were touching. He said, "What?" She said, "Nothing," but her smile opened up undiminished possibilities for them both.

The bus had started up and now it was moving faster, bouncing along down the paved county highway, between two blurred fields of soybeans.

The unifying smile was too much for her. She looked out the bus windows to where the rain was turning dirt to mud. There were raindrops on the window. He said, "You don't have to say anything. I know."

She was immediately on the offensive. "What do you know?" But he didn't need a defense. He shook his head slowly, disarming the moment that had flared accidentally in a misunderstanding. Kris realized he didn't know anything about Regina's threat. He whispered, "I know enough." Kris leaned closer to him and then pulled back a bit, enough that they wouldn't get too hot sticking together, enough so that no one would give them a hard time about being together. She said, "Good. I thought you probably did." People left Melanie and Jason alone but they'd been together forever. Everyone accepted it. As much as Regina had pressured Kris to make some declaration to Kyle, she would be the first one to call them out about getting physical on the bus. So Kris left just enough space between her and Kyle that everything could touch if either of them wanted it to. For the moment, she didn't. She just wanted them to share the privacy of the seat.

She added, "I do though, like you." He said nothing, seeming a little stunned.

She was irritated at taking the risk when he didn't have to.

He recovered quickly, knowing exactly what she needed somehow. He kneed the seat in front of them to get a rise out of Regina, who twisted around, saw them in their newfound togetherness, said, "Good. About time," and then turned right back to her absorbing chatter, leaving them to their inescapable discovery of each other.

Kris felt the mud drying against her skin. She leaned forward and found the Baggie with the witch hazel washcloth from lunch. Now dingy it was damp still. She used it on her raw weed-eaten legs, then with caution but without permission she pulled it across Kyle's arms, too. He held himself out for her to soothe that way, let her finish gently under his wrist, then traced the beds of her fingernails with his awkward fingertips.

She shook him off, needed both her hands to put the washcloth away, to fold it carefully and seal its little bag.

Once she gave up on all the anxious rustling and rearrangement of her stuff, he reached for her closest hand again. She tensed at his touch. Kris felt the totality of how it was and would be. She didn't bounce her knee, though. And Kyle didn't make fun of her, didn't pull back, or move away.

Kyle didn't move again until Kris seemed totally at ease. When she uncrossed her feet, let them dangle, he pulled her hand up to his face and ran her bent tan fingers over his cracked lips. He was right there and just steadied them both at the beginning of their forever.

THAT HOLLOW OF A POPPY STEM

Alexa grabbed her package of Miracle-Gro, slammed it down to loosen the chunks inside, and opened it. It was her day off but the date nagged at her. She knew something was happening on the twenty-third. What was it? Regardless, it was 2014, April. They were on the phone, Alexa in Chicago, Leann in their hometown, their conversation beginning on autopilot. Whatever animosity existed between them, Alexa Dirac loved her best friend Leann who had never even questioned taking her husband's name. She'd done it, the whole thing with the children, the boot-scuffing doormat, the citronella nights out back in all their favorite old lawn chairs.

Alexa fell into their familiar pattern, heard herself telling the story of what had happened. "Do you know what Ellis did when he left?"

The response from the other end was rhythmic.

"He took one of each of my earrings. Not both. Just one. Of every single pair."

The response was one of astonishment.

"I know. He's a real SOB. I finally broke down. Cried all night."

Alexa gave up on the indoor/outdoor scoop, abandoned the watering can, went directly to her walk-in closet off the bedroom. She moved purposefully out of habit. It was impossible for her to drift aimlessly, to arrive somewhere for no reason. But there she was staring at her shelves, cloistered in relative darkness for no reason. It was fine. Everything was fine. Alexa had a California closet with all the interconnected compartments.

Shoes in cubbies, sweaters folded, purses hung on pegs. The perfection of her surroundings comforted her. She could almost breathe. Her rituals were familiar, soothing. She pulled out a pair of shoes for work then realized she wasn't going to work. She said to her friend, "I just can't believe he got to me."

She did need to get dressed. In motion again, she snapped hangers from one side of the clothing bar to the other, searching. The cellphone reception wasn't always great in the closet but this morning that didn't seem to be a problem.

The laugh and the question were careful.

"Well, he did know what would really piss me off. I'll give him that." Ellis traveled for work so she had no idea where he was, what he was doing, and as of two weeks ago Thursday she couldn't ask. Right at that moment she didn't know if he were in traffic heading to his office or bypassing a TSA line at the airport. She couldn't let go of the dissipating patterns. She snapped one more hanger eight inches along the clothes bar. That did it.

Something gave way. "Shit!" She couldn't stop the bar from falling. Once the middle bar ripped out of the wall, the upper and lower bars came down as well. The whole custom closet system split apart and collapsed. Alexa reacted instinctively. She sandwiched the phone between her shoulder and ear and caught as many clothes as she could with two hands as everything sank to the floor. When the bars broke they took the perfect little stack of shelves with them. The sweaters slid off. She looked at the section of wallboard into which the shelving unit had been drilled. The screws were still perpendicular to it, still came through, the whole thing wrecked on the floor. One of the rods had snapped in half. She could see light through it.

She stood there with her heart racing, hugging an armful of clothing.

Her friend asked about the noise, asked if she were okay.

That wasn't it, Ellis leaving. It was this sickening gut feeling about what her best friend might have done. "Nothing happened," Alexa said. "They're doing construction upstairs." She tossed the clothes on top of the broken closet system, picked one dress off the top of the pile, and left the closet. She suppressed the habit of checking the day's meeting schedule on her laptop. She'd taken a few days off, which was understandable.

She needed a break. She was not going to look at her calendar.

She picked up the phone again. "But somehow Ellis knows about what went on at Olivia's wedding." She struggled out of her bathrobe, which was silky and sticking to her self-tanner, left the phone on the bed momentarily, and pulled the dress over her head. "He's gone. It's over." She charged back to the living room, carrying her shoes, letting her wet hair shake down out of a towel. If someone had been there, they'd have seen her moving with all the grace and nobility of a young queen on her coronation day. But no one was there. "You guys don't even need to come up here for the wedding. He went and called it off." She tossed the wet towel on a bar stool. "I don't mind calling my aunts. That's fine, but I'll have to call all my cousins. And. God." It was ridiculous how all her cousins, with their babies and men, were so traditional. Half of them had never even been to Lithuania. Yet at Christmas they all worried about having the right wafers for their two-year-olds. Every year Alexa got cards full of crumbs from every single relative. What was the point? Why should she take it all on herself? It's not like Ellis would get it. His family didn't even do traditions. There was no reason for her to spend five hours shopping online for old world stuff every year.

Leann, her friend, didn't even have money for fancy boutique toddler hats. She had four kids and not one of them had ever had any organic cotton anything except for what Alexa had sent. And it didn't matter. Those kids were fine.

Alexa asked, "Did you keep that little hand-crocheted christening dress I sent?"

Leann said nothing.

Alexa dropped the subject and tried to be glad she didn't have to have her kids be the ones to write *Love* in crayon and send broken bits of a shared wafer out to distant family members. It was fine. She shoved one foot into a shoe and then the other. "I'll have to call everyone, Leann." The towel had slipped off the bar stool, ended up in the watering can. Alexa yanked it out, hung it on the banana hook. "Olivia had her stupid over-the-top wedding. Charlie will never realize how much she cheats on him. What kind of sacrament is that to celebrate? Why did I even go? And now I won't even have one."

There was a question.

Alexa didn't want to have to explain. "What do you mean one what? My wedding."

Surely Leann hadn't told Ellis. It wasn't like her to go behind Alexa's back. Leann was supposed to be her best friend. But who else knew?

It didn't have to matter. It wasn't just the breakup. Something had changed in her twenty-eighth year. Suddenly Alexa found herself in constant negotiation. It wasn't only about seeing Jason at Olivia's wedding after so many years. There was always some battle of wills. It wasn't fair. Most of the deposits for the wedding preparations could still be refunded. And anyway Alexa wasn't really jealous of Leann's retractable hose on the side of the house or of the Arbor Day trees she got once a year to plant with the kids. She knew it was all a huge pain in the ass.

An hour before, though, mid-stride on her early morning lake-front run, Alexa had picked up a little turquoise and navy striped hat. It must have been cast to the ground by a furious toddler, she thought. She felt the soft ridges and laid it carefully on a nearby concrete block, hoping the child's mother kept to the same paths.

Chicago's polar vortex winter was slipping away toward sun-warmed sewer drains, and Alexa knew what her best friend had done. She damn well knew. And even if it didn't matter whose fault any of it was, she wanted to force Leann to admit it. Still, God, she didn't want that little hat getting all trampled and slushy for no reason.

So she crossed the breadth of Congress Parkway and headed home. She was in her new black body-skimming hoodie under a fitted gray vest, and she felt the compression of her black running capris—the ones with reflective okapi-like stripes. She wanted her headphones to cut her off completely. But the mental space around the sound was disturbing. Ellis, who had been the one, was no longer there burrowing into her days—with his texts, his constant voicemails, and his infuriating way of opening windows when she didn't want a draft.

It still wasn't her fault. Rapidly, her bright running shoes kept pushing her up and over the pocked asphalt. She would not panic. Wouldn't. But she forced away the sinking feeling, glad to be getting closer to home.

She was two blocks from her place and felt less ready to cry, more ready to punch a newly-installed solar-powered trash can. Her long straight ponytail swayed and swung happy-like. She made sure of it.

Tears welled up. She didn't want a confrontation with Leann, but she had to know. Something was definitely wrong.

Sunlight wedged itself between buildings and into a shadow. She didn't care how early it was in Marble Hill, Missouri, whether it were time for Leann to drive her kids to school. She had to ask her best friend, right now.

It was all over. The way it had been, the way Ellis had created for them both where she knew when he was taking off, landing, waiting for his baggage, jumping in a cab, hanging around before and after meetings, checking into hotels, finding little trinkets for her at partnered gyms, chatting about weather delays, and about time zones, about local customs—it didn't matter.

The image of him rolled over and over in her mind—always with that same damn naked smile of his, so trustworthy, happy. She remembered him hopping up when the alarm went off. No one's that happy in the morning. He was. She remembered him humming in the shower. That was what divided them, his happiness. She didn't share it, couldn't. The whole thing came apart. She remembered lying in bed hating how self-satisfied he was in it all, in their togetherness. Somehow she didn't want him to have it so easy.

Back under the steel and glass awning of her condo building, she was almost safe. The season of heat-lamps had passed but there was apparently no end to contending with salt-choked shoe tread. Just hold it together, she thought, get inside, cut a mango according to the online directions, eat it, and then call Leann. Then ask. Then know. Don't rush it. Just don't be a page out of a stupid psychology textbook. Don't obsess, don't be compulsive. Don't react. Don't respond to the idiocy of emotion, however overwhelming. Don't give all those asshole friends of his the satisfaction of a complete collapse. She forced herself to hold it together. It was fine. She just needed to stay focused: elevator, shower, nail polish, mango, call Leann.

Paul, the doorman, held the brass and glass door open for her. "Today's the day, right?" She nodded though she had no idea what he was talking about. She focused on a well-lit profusion of artificial flowers recessed in a wall of the lobby and went inside and up to her place.

Call Leann. Just do it and get it over with, just ask her.

But even if it was inevitable, it could wait a few minutes. Alexa took a moment to be comforted by what she'd managed to get for herself. Her place—her home, really—was worth all the bullshit she'd been through. She had started in interior design at Pratt, ended up finishing at The Ohio State University after her grandmother insisted she take six months off to retrieve her politicized younger cousin from some Armenian exclave in Azerbaijan. Alexa was expected to do things for everyone else but it wasn't like her grandmother was demanding this NGO-addicted cousin come and bake for Alexa for the past several weeks, get her out of bed, keep her laughing now that Ellis was gone. That girl had fallen off the face of the earth again, of course, taken in by another good cause. But it was fine. Work helped, the endless pile of paperwork on her desk, living out of a suitcase half the year, the overtime, the missed holidays, and finally not even bothering with all the imported Lithuanian traditions. It was better—this condo, this well-conceived arrangement of furniture, this living space, really.

She had a great job. A boss who couldn't go forty-eight hours without her. If that woman was in Sweden and needed an invoice? Alexa would go right to it, scan it from her phone and it would be over the Prime Meridian in two minutes. This place was worth it. Alexa paid the mortgage. (Most of the time.) So they were hers, these forty-seventh-floor windows that seemed to hold up idyllic views of Lake Michigan over light gray carpet.

The day, a white-gold blazing one now, made her squint. She didn't see the expanse of water in that moment or appreciate the reflected light. A window washer had left a streak.

She couldn't stand looking at it. She went back into the kitchen. The mangoes were in a basket by the toaster oven. She pressed buttons on the pre-programmed coffee maker.

Her coffee had a metallic tang. How many times had she told her fiance—well, her ex—not to store ground beans in that cheap canister from his mother? He never listened. She pitched the nearly full mug into the sink. Coffee splashed everywhere up to the light switch. She did not grab a sponge. She walked away, picked up her phone, and dialed her friend's familiar number. She had to know. Because, if it were true, who could do that? How could any friend do that? And if it were not true, well—

The thing with Jason at Olivia's wedding had not been totally on purpose. Things just happened. It wasn't a big deal. It shouldn't ruin everything.

If she and Leann were speaking in person, they'd been friends long enough that any glance would tell Alexa all she needed to know. But it was hard to parse the truth from so far away. She pulled on some dead leaves of the philodendron. The stems weren't quite dry enough that she could snap them off. She grabbed her kitchen scissors and clipped away what had already started to decay. But then it hit her again. She jammed the shears back in the wooden block.

If Alexa were there, though, back home, Leann would recognize how wrong she had been. Alexa would go right over there, pound on the door, rip that stupid Easter wreath off the door, toss it out in her mother's azalea bushes, charge in there and scream right in her face. Leann wouldn't even know what was coming. Alexa was angry enough to just about put her in a chokehold and make her wish she'd never opened her mouth.

But Alexa wasn't back home to make her best friend pay for the transgression. It was all so simple. Leann probably hadn't said a word to Ellis, had probably just messaged him on Facebook. Actions were so slight these days and reactions could be so disproportionate. Alexa didn't want to be that way; she wanted to maintain a measured calm. Still, it was unforgivable. They were supposed to be friends. The thought of that little toddler's hat waiting on the cement block came back to her. Would the child's mother find it? She wanted her to find it, to get it back, to have everything come together instead of falling apart. She was sick of having everything destroyed. She shoved the dead leaves down the garbage disposal, flipped the switch on, and then off, quickly. Just a vorticose burst of blades.

She had to know. She grabbed her phone, thumbed down through her contacts, pressed the picture of Leann's new blue heeler, and the phone rang in Missouri—Leann always took forever to pick up—

Now Leann didn't allow herself a real reaction when the phone rang. She knew it was Alexa. Because only one person ever called this early and only ever when there was some kind of problem, and there was always a problem. With the resignation of those consigned to the multiple duties of this life, Leann picked up her telephone, and searched for her glasses. She fell into the familiar pattern of their chat with, "Hey girl. What happened?"

She didn't need to say much to flush out her friend out like some quarry under the gun. Just a couple words and it came tumbling toward her, the truth. She said, "No, what'd he do?"

She cradled the telephone and searched again with her hands for her glasses. They weren't on the windowsill where she usually left them. She leaned forward over the sink and looked behind the ceramic frog, the soap dish, the copper scrubber, and the neck of the faucet. Leann knew her best friend well enough that she could almost see her pacing around her condo, cooling down after her run.

Even if she was off by fifteen minutes, she was pretty much right. They really were best friends. Her side of the conversation that morning took place in a little Missouri kitchen where she could wipe splatters of cherry juice off the butter-yellow semi-gloss walls. But harvesting the cherries from that row of trees along the fence-line would still be another six weeks.

She didn't remember what christening dress Alexa was talking about. When had that been? It was a blur. Leann couldn't even focus on the piece of paper in her hand: evicted. How could such a thing happen to her family? She had a husband working full-time, had kids, had everything on neat shelves in the shed. It wasn't possible. The kids were next door, likely swirling in a fury and watching cartoons, gleeful that school would be starting a few hours late with a fog delay. They were on heightened alert, though, ready to go whenever she called them. The eviction notice wasn't all that threatening, just a piece of paper. But, God, she didn't want to lose her homes, she wanted to have friends over again to pick and pit cherries, wanted to laugh, holler at each other over nothing, clear away layers of soggy newspaper folded up around all the hand-torn pits and stems, dripping juice all the way to the trash can. She wanted to have another cherry cobbler with ice cream for the neighbors. She did not want this foreclosure upon her home.

But for Alexa—at least for the moment—the thing about whether her friend had been the one to tell

Ellis wasn't worth belaboring. She knew Leann was totally disempowered, had only finished three years of a degree in corporate communications at Southeast Missouri State in Cape Girardeau when her husband made her quit. Who could live that way? That totally diminished sense of self wasn't healthy. Alexa said nothing but mocked her friend's tone internally as she replayed the wonted, "Oh my gosh. What was that? Are you okay?" Of course she was okay. It was just a closet bar.

Alexa's doorbell rang. Who could it be? It was still pretty early. It had to be Ellis. He'd canceled his meetings for the day and come home. He loved her, they'd figure it out, the earrings would be together again. They'd be together again, the problems would not be a big deal, and she'd get to marry him, to live with him in his amazing place—which really was better than hers—and she'd have that car, that designer trench coat she wanted, that trip to Switzerland they'd talked about, the quilted headboard, the butler's pantry, the diversified investment portfolio, the insurance, the matching jet skis—all of it.

She just about leapt to the door, just about hung up on her friend. But at the same time, since she knew it was Ellis, she didn't want to seem too eager, too thrilled.

Let him knock again. She'd be cool and offhand. She'd just open the door, nod, motion for him to come in, and then make him wait while she kept talking to Leann.

After the second knock, she pulled the door open. It wasn't Ellis.

She was confused. It was two guys, one of them with a two-wheel dolly. She stared at them, very glad she'd already put on a dress.

For an instant she was worried they were repo men. But no, most of her pieces were floor models from the design studio where she worked. The rest was paid for, mostly. Slowly, then in a panoptic rush, she realized they were the movers she and Ellis had hired. Alexa was in shock. Oh Jesus. That's what was happening on the twenty-third of April. The movers were coming to take her stuff over to Ellis's two weeks before the wedding.

The plan had been such a good one two months ago. She wouldn't have to be bothered to meet the movers at her condo. But now? They were ready to take everything she owned. There was a language barrier but it didn't matter. She didn't say a word. The deposit had been paid. Paul downstairs had let them in. It was all playing out exactly as they'd arranged.

She realized that anyone else would probably have sent the movers away immediately. She should have. Right then. Should have just said, "Thanks for making the trip but your services are no longer required," flipped the deadbolt, and called Paul to make them go away. But she had arranged the whole thing. She was the one who had picked the day, made the appointment. Alexa said, "Oh my God."

One of the guys handed her a work order.

She was trapped.

She held the phone as though holding her best friend's hand.

God knew what Ellis would do later that night when he got home and found all her stuff in his place. He would probably go ballistic, burn everything in a pyre with her effigy tied to a stake. Or, more likely given his disposition, he would be sensible, sell everything he could and have a donation center pick up the rest.

The discussions with the owner of the moving company flooded back to her. She and Ellis had been so demanding, so adamant about how efficient the crew had to be, and how they absolutely would not get paid one dime until the move was completed to their satisfaction.

It was all contractual. Ellis's lawyer had set it up with the lawyer of the moving company. Alexa and her ex-fiancé were not people who left things to chance. There was no trust in the space between them and the world. None. So at this point, the move couldn't be undone just by waving the guys off with a couple of twenties and explaining that the situation had changed. She vaguely remembered how she'd screamed into the telephone about how much hell there'd be to pay if any duct tape adhesive ended up anywhere on the varnish of her favorite armoire. And she remembered what color Ellis had turned when his lawyer said the moving company would include their belongings in a truck with the belongings of another couple in the same neighborhood, to save fuel costs on both jobs. Ellis said no. Ellis told the lawyer to tell the moving company's lawyer that under no circumstance were their possessions to be commingled with anyone else's. The money for the movers was tied up in escrow, the lawyer's, too. There were line items of pointed instruction about how to wrap the pieces, what packing materials to use, and how not to jostle the two large vases that framed her entry.

It was fine. Getting more furniture wouldn't be a problem. Her boss was always dumping floor samples in the alley behind the store if no one wanted them. And there was Craigslist. All this stuff reminded her of Ellis anyway. Let him have it. It wasn't a decision, really. She took the work order and smiled without meaning it. It was as good as done. They were through the door and busying themselves. One of the guys seemed disgruntled that she wasn't already packed. In two minutes he had gone down in the elevator and come back up with three more guys who must have been waiting in the truck. They had boxes and a platform dolly.

They started taking everything.

As she stood there, helpless, everything was working exactly as planned. The truth was she wanted an answer from Leann more than she wanted to stop these men from taking all her stuff.

Alexa said, "Are you still there?"

Leann muttered yes and the conversation spun on. "So. Okay," Alexa continued. "The point is, I didn't think finding his keys on my wet bar was a big deal because he leaves his stuff everywhere. I've had to take his wallet to him at work I don't know how many times. And remember when he had to have the hotel in the Solomon Islands FedEx his phone back?"

Alexa sort of did want to tell Leann that these guys were invading her home, not helping to create a new one the way they should have been. Whatever was happening to her expectations about her future, the movers were there, working. She'd have to deal with all the people she knew at some point. But she could not deal with these men judging her for how she demanded that they be so careful with everything, and then turn around and say the whole job was unnecessary. She couldn't do it. Let them take whatever they wanted. Let them put it wherever they thought it should go.

She knew she'd never get any of it back.

She watched as they took the utmost care with all her possessions. They were doing a great job. But it didn't matter.

She wasn't about to cry, but illusions weren't as robust as hopes. These strangers didn't care about her life. They just had a pickup address and a delivery location.

The men took end tables, bar stools, and both sofas while Alexa's voice grew more tense.

Not knowing the whole of the situation, of how the movers were taking everything right then, her best friend—whose home faced a similar fate—got a little impatient, must have said something snide.

Alexa couldn't quite tell: had Leann told Ellis? The only way to know for sure was to ask. Alexa didn't want to lose it in front of the movers. Still, it was unforgivable. She wasn't paranoid, she knew.

"Can I ask you something?" Alexa blurted out suddenly.

Back in her own kitchen, Leann stretched the telephone cord across the countertop ruining stacks of bills and a child's arrangement of blue plastic toys.

She wasn't really paying attention to the conversation but she took her cue. "Of course."

She opened the refrigerator and leaned all the way in, squinting to look at an expiration date. She grabbed the milk, the eggs, and the tub of margarine. She set the milk carton on the counter so that the picture of the missing child could not accost her. Even without her glasses she knew about that pixilated blur.

But she also knew her friend would back off. And she did. They were talking about the earrings thing again. "I know how much you love your earrings. He shouldn't have done that."

The sun peeked out. There was no more fog. This happened a lot. The school would make the call, announce on the radio that classes would begin late, and then the fog would lift. The rhythm of unmet expectations was no disruption for Leann. What did it matter if the day began two hours later than usual? Who knew what the conditions were like ten miles further out? Fog often did obscure curves in country roads. No rumble strips on their shoulders, just rises and ravines, couldn't have the school buses out blind in that. So let the kids have their fun next door. Their homework was done.

She kept the radio on, though, half-listening for the next announcement, which would no doubt say the kids should be going within the hour.

Her friend kept talking. Leann moved over to the cabinets, stretching the cord again. She opened the bottom cabinet and jumped back. There was a dead mouse in the trap. She made no sound, didn't want to interrupt her friend's story. Quietly she collected herself, leaned close again, squinting, and gingerly picked up the trap by the edges. She walked across the kitchen to the trash, stepped on the plastic pedal to pop the greasy white lid, and dropped the whole mess into the can.

"Were all the earrings from him?"

Leann opened a kitchen drawer. She pulled a new wooden mousetrap from a plastic package and set it on the counter. She ignored how her linoleum was curling up at the baseboards and how a dirty film left by mop water had collected in hundreds of tiny shallow pits. She got a jar of peanut butter. She used a piece of a saltine to dip out just a bit of the bait and took a fingerful for herself. Worried she might be blind at sixty-five, she leaned really close to the counter while cradling the phone on her shoulder. She readied the trap with the saltine and stood up.

"It's nice when a guy actually does give gifts. He's pretty generous with you or was." Her husband had bought her a new transmission last October, said that was the present for her birthday and Christmas.

It was enough.

Leann's feet were hot, sweaty, so she kicked her slippers toward the sliding door. They landed on the mat near a pair of dirty work boots and a shiny pair of bright purple rain boots. Then, thinking about mice, Leann went and put the slippers back on again. With her slippered toe she straightened both pairs of boots against the edge of the mat.

"When'd he do this?"

Back at the counter she picked up the mousetrap, opened her cabinet door, and placed it in a prime location among the stockpots—close but not exactly where the other trap had been. She picked up a non-stick skillet and noticed a long scratch in its surface. One of the kids must have cut a pancake in half with a metal knife. Shaking her head she walked toward the carport and opened the door wide enough to toss the frying pan into the large cardboard box marked, "Goodwill." The screen door caught her foot when it snapped shut. She winced, again suppressing her reaction so her friend's story could go on.

"He put his keys on the floor during the Symphony?"

"Why the hell would he do that?"

Leann sat down and squinted at her foot—no skin broken. She rubbed it until the pain receded. Held her breath, counted to ten in her mind, the way she taught her kids to do. And it worked for her as well as it did for them. When she got to eight the throbbing pain was gone.

"Well, what happened with the earrings? You're way off track."

The slipper had dropped outside onto the cold cement when the screen door snapped shut. She needed it. She leaned out the door and picked up her slipper from where it had fallen. The screen door squeaked.

"Why did he even take his cellphone overseas? Weren't you guys supposed to be on vacation?"

Leann went to the drawer with the mousetraps and rummaged around with one hand until she found a little can of oil. 3-IN-ONE, it said. She returned to the screen door and tested it, listening for where the squeak originated. Leaning close and concentrating on the hinge, she moved the door back and forth with her slippered foot.

"What were you thinking? Weren't you upset?"

Pinpointing the spot, she pulled the little red conical cap off the oil and applied a few drops to the offender. Before putting the lid back on, she worked the door some more with her foot. Satisfied that the squeak was eradicated, she shoved the tip of the can back into the pointed red cap in her mouth, carried the oil back across the kitchen, and left it on the counter.

"But he hit below the belt. You love your earrings."

She looked for her glasses again under a stack of catalogs and coupons. She began sorting the catalogs, then, disgusted, giving up, dropped them by heaps into the trashcan.

"Doesn't he have some stuff over at your place? Maybe you can talk things over when he comes back for it." Laughing. "Well, so what now? Where do things stand?"

She opened the oven door and pulled out her cast-iron skillet. She went back to the refrigerator, and with a spoon got a dollop of bacon grease from a mug. The white blob fell into the black skillet. She turned the flame on really low and let the grease go clear.

"What rhinestone earrings?"

The kids hadn't eaten yet; likely wouldn't have at the neighbor's house either. She took out a ceramic bowl, set it in the sink, and cracked seven eggs into it. She laid the shells aside on a plastic cutting board to keep the albumin off the counter. The salt and pepper shakers were just out of reach. She missed only a few seconds of Alexa's story when she put down the phone and went to grab them. A few dashes of salt went in the bowl, a lot more pepper, and then the little kissing bears were returned to the stove. The phone was back on her shoulder in an instant as Leann felt behind the napkin holder for her glasses.

"But then what? My God."

She poured the milk into the bowl but did not measure it.

Standing at the sink she looked again for her glasses. She ran her hand all along the windowsill and even stood on tiptoe to see if somehow they had gotten between the sash and the storm window.

"How could he know? How—how did he find out?"

Leann picked up the bowl and whisked the eggs with the fork, quicker and quicker. "You're not missing anything."

Thinking ahead into the next hour, she picked up a tiny doll that needed to go back to her daughter's room. She dropped it into the pocket of her apron and heard it clank against her glasses. They were right there in that pocket the whole time.

"I'd love it if you could," she said. "We'd all love to see you. I'm not glad the wedding's off. I'm so sorry. But it's just not a good time with the last month of school." It wasn't enough of a reason. Leann added, "The pullout couch is broken anyway." She kept adding reasons, beginning a wall where none had been. "We're having our carpets steam cleaned. Gene's brother said he'd do it while we were in Chicago but now he wants to get it done this weekend instead of next. It's going to be too chaotic." And then because that wasn't enough either, really, she added a final, "Plus, come on, Alexa. What's the point? Even if you're down here, you won't let any of us in."

Astounded pout.

Leann put on her glasses, turned off the burner and sat down at the kitchen table. She still cradled the phone to her ear. "Honey, we all want answers. I'd be doing very well to find one matched pair of earrings myself with these kids always rummaging through everything I own and losing half of it. But what're you gonna do? They all need to eat and somewhere to sleep 'til they're eighteen." She picked up the eviction notice again and began reading it while listening to her friend.

They would have had thirty days if she had opened the mail three weeks ago. Now what did they have? She didn't want to think about it and didn't have to. Confrontation was unnecessary, and Alexa never had to know. Ellis had called out of nowhere, caught her completely off guard, and asked her point-blank. What was she supposed to say?

Her friend must have protested in some unspoken way, to the comment about not letting her in.

Outside, through the bit of fog that had returned somehow, the backyard willow revealed itself, shrouded in its chartreuse veil that hung—hung on—in windless weather.

Leann said, "I promise," and took off her glasses again, laid them on the table pinched her nose. Her friend didn't want to let go, wouldn't hang up. They stayed there together in a moment of long-distance silence, clinging to something of a shared past. Leann leaned her chin on her hand, remembering. She thought about the whole youth group floating down the river on tractor-tire inner tubes as kids, thought about a trip to the mall with their bangs up high, and wondered whatever happened to that broken-heart best friend necklace.

Stupid kid stuff. Junk from some kiosk at the mall. There were never two halves to any whole heart.

But Alexa was in a different place with it. Leann always had that soft touch on Alexa's heart. That gentle way of leading her home from nowhere. So Alexa didn't care so much who was right, or wrong. It just wasn't fair. None of it. She got back to the earrings. "No. They weren't all from him. He gave me maybe five pairs. The diamond studs, for Christmas the first year we were together when he was still trying to impress me. Another, the gold dangly ones, for my birthday two years ago—and then remember the ones I wore with the green dress to Olivia's wedding, from those pictures I sent you? Those big drop pearls? Those ones. And I think he brought me some turquoise and silver ones from a business trip to Santa Fe. The little stainless steel stars were for fun last August after we went boating one night. He would not shut up about being out together under the sky. There were the antique rubies—I loved those—he gave me that pair the night I met his parents. So I guess six pairs, not five. Oh. And, of course, the pavé diamond hoops. So seven."

There was astonishment and then a question.

"Yes. That pair was definitely my favorite. And. He took both of those. I'm not sure why. Probably to return them. I have no idea when he was here. Sometime while I was at work, most likely. He knew better than to start some shit with me home. Chicken shit. All I know is there was no note or anything. I just got home and his set of keys to my place was on the wet bar by the door. I guess the busy pattern in that gorgeous piece of hibiscus oil cloth—remember, the one I brought back from Mexico?—obscured them at first. I set down a bag of groceries and heard something. I just figured he'd forgotten them like always.

The emotional response was questioned.

Alexa left the plants and went to the doorway of her bedroom. The movers were getting industrious. One was in her walk-in closet dumping the heap of clothes into a refrigerator-sized box. Two others were dismantling the bed. Alexa stood stunned in the doorway, watching them, and kept talking to Leann. "You're right. I don't know why it didn't affect me right away. I guess because I was a little bit in shock. And I didn't really know what it meant. I knew he had done it, taken one of each, but I didn't think about it. I guess I was hurrying so much that it didn't sink in. Only hit me when I took these days off." She watched the strangers destroying the place where she and Ellis had spent so many nights together.

They were efficient. One of them eased the mattress onto the carpet and slipped the slats out of the side rails. He pulled the footboard away, laid it down carefully. Started wrapping it in quilted blankets just as dictated by the contract. Duct-taping the whole thing. They were gentle but not cautious, knowing their work, trusting their hands. They didn't care but still they did protect this heirloom of some family none of them had known. The guy working on the mattress was just as quick to carry out his orders. He had a plastic bag, a huge one. He laid it out and got it ready. Alexa couldn't breathe.

A point needed to be clarified.

She was awash in the fact that all this was happening. For an instant she pictured herself in that plastic bag, completely encased, duct tape choking her, wrists bound behind her back, her body forgotten under a dumpster. She finally didn't fight. Couldn't cry out. Felt it futile to scream. She just held herself together with the familiarity of friendly conversation. "Yeah. I know. I did find one pair to wear. I had my grandma's pearl studs in the console of my car."

Another point needed to be clarified.

"He has a few things here but not a lot. I think maybe a pair of cargo shorts and a sweatshirt. He won't come back for those. He doesn't care about clothes. Probably doesn't even know they're here." She didn't explain that in two hours Ellis would have all his clothes and most of hers, too. Who cared? Alexa pushed away the thought of herself under that dumpster, kept her voice steady. "He took both the pavé diamond hoops though. And then he did something else, too. Just low. I'll tell you in a minute." Leann might have been compassionate. "Yeah. He was the one, if you believe in all that."

The mover with the quilted blankets had finished with the headboard. The guy dealing with the mess in the walk-in closet had placed the huge box and the plastic wrapped bedframe on a platform dolly. He maneuvered the unwieldy bulk out through the doorway. Alexa had to get out from under that dumpster in her mind. She focused on herself and Leann as little girls in matching dresses twirling with their fistfuls of poppies, barefoot in the new spring grass, posing, arching their backs, jutting out their hips, hanging doll clothes on scale-model clotheslines, just like grown-ups.

They were too much like grown-ups when they were young and so like children as adults.

Alexa didn't want the wall she heard begin in Leann's voice. She remembered not only the moment of their twirling with the poppies. It was that next moment, being five, six, or seven, throwing all but one flower onto the grass, clutching that last poppy stem, feeling the hairs on it, stroking it, holding it up, being pretty, twirling, but then stopping abruptly and, for no reason crushing the stem, ripping it to shreds, to feel it happening, to make the thing come undone. She also recalled that moment of peer pressure—one little girl still twirling, still pretty, the other saying, "Stop. Do this. Snap it," while demonstrating destruction.

Only the mattress was left in the bedroom. It was there on the floor. The movers didn't hesitate. One of the guys grabbed the big plastic bag as the other flipped the mattress on its side. They would have begun packaging the thing immediately but one of them stopped and said, "Wait. What is that?"

The other guy knelt and motioned for Alexa to come closer, to see what he'd found.

She could tell he was thrilled, eager to show something to her. When she got close enough, she could see it lying there in the palm of his hand—that second pavé diamond hoop.

So Ellis had not taken both. He had taken one, and the other had been there all the time, lost under their bed.

She froze. She pretended the man held nothing and spoke into the phone deliberately, as if what faced her—that little lost earring—had nothing to do with who she was, with whatever meaning had snapped between her and Ellis. She didn't care. She said to Leann, "All I know is that I want to have Christmas dinner again. That I want my mother to have a place to come for Thanksgiving. That's why I bought this condo instead of looking at places like his third floor walk-up on his precious leafy street. It's not like we're all fated to some earthly hell. I'm no home-and-hearth goddess. It never would have worked with him anyway. I want Mom to have access, to have that elevator, to be able to visit in five and ten years. No matter how feeble and frail she gets I want her to be able to get into my home. Ellis doesn't have an elevator. You know? But, fuck, my mom should be able to get in the door. And I just want to be able to get my groceries inside and maybe maneuver a stroller into my own place. Easily, you know?"

Alexa felt a surge of fury because of the moving guys. They were staring at her, not even embarrassed, listening in on her phone conversation though she couldn't tell how much they understood. But something held her back from launching into a full-blown tirade. Not pride, not decorum. It was that contract. She stared at the pavé diamond hoop in the moving guy's hand.

She couldn't acknowledge it, couldn't take it from him, couldn't tell him what to do with it. He stayed there kneeling but looked at his boss, who shrugged. Alexa went on talking to Leann, kept staring at the earring in the moving guy's hand. "It's like I have all these pieces, I try to come at it from all these angles, and I can't assemble it. The whole thing—marriage, home, kids, family—it crumbles. I feel like I've been trying to build something ever since I dated Jason. Prom and all that. All the stupid hopes of kids who don't know any better. I didn't know I had all these idiot dreams about it all. Did you? But I remember meeting Jason's mother and being like, 'Okay. This is the real thing. This woman could be my mother-in-law.' I was aware of that when she was handing me a kitchen knife and telling me to dice two onions for the meatloaf. I did it. I diced those onions just like she told me. Perfectly. But that was it. I never went back. And. Time after time it just does not work. And now it's not going to work with Ellis.

She could almost see the movers showing up at his place with all her stuff. She imagined herself and Ellis laughing about what a terrible misunderstanding it had been.

And then she imagined what it would do to Ellis when that mover handed him the one last earring.

Without that earring, the confusion about the movers was sweet, was innocent. The two of them fumbling along together. Without that earring, he might accept her back or might not. Maybe they could see a therapist, work through it. But the uncertainty of letting him decide was too hard. Just let it be over. He'd been the one to take her earrings. He should be the one to suffer. She choked on a swell of remorse. She looked at the hole in the wall in the closet where the bar had come down.

She motioned for the moving guy to stand up, to get off his knees. She couldn't take the earring but she didn't want him looking at her like that anymore either. She turned her back on him, shut the closet door, and continued her conversation. "Leann?" Her friend was there, was listening. "Last night I had this dream. I was in some inventor's workshop in a snowy country, way out in the middle of nowhere, where the snow isn't even plowed. They had to tunnel through it to keep the roads open. Fine. So. There was a guy there, and there was this little bird, orange, white, and black. Not a phoenix. The opposite. It kept dying mid-flight. Very small, maybe only four inches long. Tiny, really, like a hummingbird. But the bird was hovering right there in the workshop. It kept rising and then beating its wings and falling. As it fell, the wings broke, the feathers molted off, and it disintegrated in the air—right as it tried to stay aloft. But somehow it made it to the zenith of its abilities over and over and as it did so, its little wings were fine again, fully-feathered, lovely.

"It just kept happening. In slow motion. I watched it, mesmerized. That bird wasn't me. I didn't feel any strong connection the way you do sometimes when the meaning in life piles up and really, really matters, is some kind of spirit of your own in others. It didn't matter that much. The bird was apart from me, living its own cyclic hell. But I couldn't do anything for it, neither could the inventor. But, Leann, the inventor didn't care. That was Ellis. I know it. He turned away from the bird. I couldn't. I felt like someone should at least be aware of what was happening with it. So I was its witness, watching it rot in flight like that, in this guy's amazing place."

The movers were getting impatient. Alexa didn't want any loose ends though, no open doors. Just finish it.

She held the cellphone away, looked directly at the mover with the earring, and said, "Make sure he gets that with the rest."

The mover slowly closed his hand around the earring, like a hurt child treasuring a butterfly.

The other mover didn't think much of her decision, that was obvious. But in the way they'd been instructed to wrap the heirloom headboard, they would deliver the earring. Still, the mover had his judgment about how she was handling things. He waved his arm, mumbled something in another language, and the two men sealed the mattress in the plastic, took it away toward the freight elevator, and were gone.

Alexa fled the bedroom, paced the hall for a few moments, walked in a circle in her kitchen, and then ended up in the living room. There was a sound in Missouri, in Leann's home, over the phone.

"Was that a mousetrap? What are you doing?" Alexa asked, but she didn't wait for an answer. "The only earrings Ellis did not take were the rhinestone ones. They were the ones Jason got me when we went to the prom together. Tacky, really, but grown-up-looking, you know. Something to feel dressed up in—tin foil pretty much—but a little bit elegant. They were both in the jewelry box—right there together. Only they weren't where I had put them. I had them tucked away forever kind of hidden in a little Asian embroidered pouch. I don't even know why I kept them; I'd never wear them now. Just a keepsake, I guess. Well somehow Ellis must have found out about me sleeping with Jason at Olivia's wedding. Because instead of that pair being tucked away, those crappy earrings from prom were lying side by side right in the middle of the second drawer of the jewelry box."

Shock. Disapproval.

It wasn't that Alexa said a word about her furniture disappearing or that Leann admitted her family was being thrown out of their home. But still they shared the void. "I know. What am I going to do, Leann? We were supposed to move in together this week. Today. I don't even know how to deal with canceling all the wedding stuff. Mom's completely clueless. She keeps tying dried lavender in tulle thinking everything's fine. I'm going to have to tell her but I don't know how. She's already imagined three grandchildren, with presents under the tree every year til she's dead. So damn hopeful. What am I supposed to do?"

They were no longer defenders of the hearth.

Neither were they little fourth grade girls anymore being told it's best to love a world by stuffing slips of paper—names of individual pediatric cancer patients—into balloons to release from a hospital rooftop. That that's what to do. That that's how to show others matter, that you care. That that's enough of an action to take, facing death with colored balloons. There was none of that. None of the way things should be. Entropy swiped away the reasons. Alexa put her hand on the tall window, reached out toward the city below, toward the lake, toward that cloud-covered horizon.

There was a quiet moment. Neither of them cared that their homes were dismantled. They did. But, not the way you're supposed to with deference to the head of the household, with meek persistence, with every moment devoted to three jobs, two mortgages, endless toil, confident pride, and a white-picket heroism, undefeated. Instead, Alexa sat down cross-legged on the floor. The movers had left several dead leaves on the gray carpet. She picked up a leaf, cracked it between her forefinger and her thumb, and ran her fingernail along the spine of the particularly large stem. "Can I come stay with you for a week or so? I just need to be home somewhere."

She helped the brittle thing come apart while listening to her best friend's refusal piling up. She choked, put her hand back on that window glass, then gave up totally, leaned her forehead against it, looked down at the nearest swimming pool still covered with a taut tarp, at a rooftop garden coming back to life. It was someone's tax deduction, someone's contribution to the way things should be, someone's pride and joy likely showed off to giggling dates who probably weren't allowed to be up there.

She had to have her friend. "Well, so leave the kids with your mom for a few days and come up here. Doesn't Marble Hill get old? We can have a spa day, get our hair done. Get some wine. I just really need to see you."

The question was calculated, though careful and kind.

Alexa was sensitive to the piteous tone of it. She jerked away from the glass, collected herself, jumped up, grabbed each of the dead leaves off the floor, stood firm, looking out over the entire city. She drew power from the east-west boulevards, from the parks greening up, from a weather helicopter banking north. "I don't know how he found out." She did know. It was over, their savored friendship. There was no balloon release from any rooftop. Alexa walked to the sink and threw the dead leaves down the disposal, thinking maybe she heard a little remorse mixed with her friend's empathy. That did it. With all the inflexibility of Atropos she fell forward into the impossible hell of what was most likely true.

"You told him about Jason, didn't you?"

THE NIGHTMARE STATE OF LEDUC

Mrs. Givand told her husband, "He didn't bring it in because I wouldn't let him go outside." She yawned. It was still early. "He had a fever of 102 degrees three days ago and the past two days it's been raining. The truck and the piggy bank are separate issues, John." Mrs. Givand leaned against the exposed brick wall. She was eight months pregnant.

Their son, Matthew, age three, had followed his mother downstairs but was steering clear of his father. The child planted himself on the couch on the other side of the kitchen's old porch wall. During the remodel, the Givands had kept as many original elements as they could. The choice had been not to brick up the old living room windows but to leave them weathered and working, for charm. Two-penny nails at the limits of each sash stopped the old wooden porch windows from sliding out of their tracks. The couch on the other side was a safe vantage for Matthew, who turned on the TV to establish his presence. He played with the mute button. The sound of cartoons came and went without rhythm.

Matthew should have known better. But he was still too little. His mother had seen him slip her wedding rings through the piggy bank slot just like pennies. And now they wouldn't slip out down a knife blade, or appear anywhere on top of all the coins so that they could be pulled out with tweezers. Shadows inside the ceramic pig made it impossible to see. Using a flashlight didn't help. They'd tried the LED keychain light, the big one for changing tires in an emergency, and the regular one with a dim flickering beam. If they turned the piggy bank upside down, then all the pennies lay across the slot. Light couldn't shine in at all.

One section of the low porch wall and three of the lovely hewn pillars made an island where they'd worked for two futile hours, fumbling, finagling—

fixating. So there they were, the three of them.

The house had been in Mrs. Givand's family for three generations. The young couple had purchased the property from her grandmother right before her grandfather died. They'd worked so hard on the place, to make it exactly what they thought it should be. Mrs. Givand looked at her husband and said, "Let's do it in the sink."

John Givand, thirty-five, was growing his first beard. So far he'd impressed no one with it. His wife tolerated whatever phase he was going through. His mother thought he should shave it off and stop drawing attention to himself with such childish nonsense during his wife's second pregnancy. His son said it was scratchy. And his friends at work made cracks about lumberjack hipsters. But the beard wasn't the focus right then. John hugged the huge Delft piggy bank to his chest. He went to the sink but seemed worried at his wife's suggestion, as if his own father would find out. "You think so?"

"Yes. Otherwise it will make a mess everywhere. And not outside. I don't want any ceramic shards in the grass."

John looked toward the old detached garage. It

was covered with ivy. "So the sink?"

Their son's head popped up over the back of the couch. Matthew knew something had happened and that it was his fault. The only defense he had against his suffocating shame was the pressure of his little finger on the remote's mute button.

His pregnant mom moved slowly into the hall to a linen closet and brought back their best big bath towel, the new one. It was the color of some insignia for the merchant marine, a deep navy blue. Offering this towel as a liner for the sink was a gesture of significance. Matthew knew it. He continued to turn the TV volume off and on, off and on.

Mr. Givand seemed partially appeased by the choice of the best towel and held the piggy bank at the ready.

Mrs. Givand opened the cabinet below the sink and pulled out a scouring pad and cleaning powder. Her son and husband watched as she scrubbed away hard water stains, rubbed the faucet handles to gleaming and sopped up the filmy soap scum which had collected around the fixture.

It was just a bath towel, a high-end one bought at

a discount department store. But Mrs. Givand lent some majesty to the cloth, as might be lent to draperies darkening 12th century castles or to the curved fabric rumples hiked up on the marble laps of great statues.

Mrs. Givand took her time, smoothed the towel and pressed its thickness into all the corners of the sink with both hands. The textured edges rose out onto the counter. She anchored them with heavy objects. It was an appropriately prepared altar.

John Givand hesitated. It was as if the ceramic pig were alive and kicking in his hands, with its haunches trembling, its head tossing in terror.

Mrs. Givand moved behind her husband, leaned her forehead into the space between his shoulder blades, said nothing. She wrapped her hands around his chest, holding on with firm assurance. They both felt the new baby kick.

The ceramic pig did not need to be stunned. No one shaved the right spot for an electrode. John just set the old Delft thing down on that soft navy towel in the sink, gently.

Mrs. Givand looked at her son. "Turn those cartoons off, Matthew. This is not the time for television."

Matthew hated being told what to do. He turned the volume up loud, threw the remote on the couch, left the TV blaring, ran up the burgundy carpeted stairs, threw open two doors upstairs, and let the morning rush in through the Juliet balcony. Dissatisfied instantly, however, with the ivy, with the old wrought iron door that scraped against the ceiling and floor, he pounded back down the stairs, landing on each one loud and hard, and went right back to the TV room and turned off the noise before his father had another chance to yell.

The silence engulfed what ire had begun to escalate.

John Givand placed the piggy bank carefully in the towel-lined sink. "Four generations." He thought about his grandfather who had bought the piggy bank for his son. He thought about his dad as a child putting in his coins.

John had a flash of memory from a moment when he was seventeen. He had wrecked the Sterling, just dinged the paint job, really, and he and his father were not speaking. He was in his room reading and he remembered how his mother opened the door—didn't look at him at all, not knowing what to say—but walked right over to the piggy bank on the windowsill. She had Windex and some paper towels. For several minutes she worked to clean the piggy bank. Then she left the room without saying a word. John remembered apologizing to his father about wrecking the car later that evening when his old man got home from work. He'd faced it, like a son had to, like a man. But only because his mother had done that, had reminded him of the significance. How could he break this thing open after all of that?

A burst of breeze knocked a doorknob against the wall in the upstairs hallway.

The TV sound flipped back on. Mrs. Givand ignored her child, rubbed her husband's back. "Remember your dad, honey? How excited he was to give this to you?" Her voice had the tone of a eulogy. "He was so happy about Matthew coming."

John remembered the smells of mildewed insulation and hot wood. He felt the two-by-fours under his feet.

"Dad kept joking that I'd fall through those attic stairs." There was a pause. The TV went mute again. The breeze had become light and they all strained to hear the quiet rap of the doorknob against the wall upstairs, the old blown glass shifting in windowsills all over the house. "That smile he had. I never saw him so happy as when he brought this thing to the house the day we brought Matthew home from the hospital."

Now, three years later, clouds scudded across the April morning sky. It was irrational to hate his own son, to hate having to preserve the meaning of wedding rings. He almost suggested they buy her another set, but no, she wouldn't go for it. He knew he had to break the thing open. But not yet. "I don't think anyone's ever been that happy."

"John. We can get another ring."

He looked at her, almost saved by her grace. "You want your grandmother's diamond in my grandfather's piggy bank forever? That's ridiculous."

"Why is it ridiculous? Maybe that's how it should be."

"What? That's how it should be because a three-year-old decided so on an impulse? No, honey. No."

She listened to her husband tell the familiar story.

"When I was a kid I asked grandpa why he hadn't smelled the eggs spoiling on the ship, in the crate. He said that there were so many nasty smells on that ocean liner that he just turned his face into the wind and hadn't even noticed. They were all smokers then anyway. And who knows what time of year it was? Could have been plenty cool to keep the eggs fresh. He loved telling that story." John looked down into the sink. "He would hate this."

"You just said it had to be done."

John looked at his wife, looked at the old detached garage, put his hand on the side of the pig, but told the story for his son, who knew something was his in the moment, and turned the TV all the way off. John said, "Grandpa worked on Wall Street. As a kid he ran messages from banks to men's clubs, worked his way up. Never went to college, proved himself by his word and his raw talent for numbers. He could count money faster than anyone in New York. Won those contests they had, got a job higher up. Took an ocean liner to Europe on business at some point. He'd been in Holland for a week and had a day off, went for that walk. He never admitted as much, but Grandma said he got lost and couldn't remember the name of his hotel. He never conceded the point, always said he was just out for a walk to enjoy the sights. Regardless of whether he were lost, he stopped in a little shop. He said this piggy bank was there behind the counter. He just said, 'The damned thing looked me square in the eye, unnerved me. But after all those years of running messages, I knew to respect anyone that looks you in the eye that way.'

"So he bought the pig right off the shelf and had to get it crated up by an egg vendor. They didn't have any UPS store or Styrofoam peanuts back then. Grandpa figured it out, made sure it got all the way back across the ocean with him, safe and sound. I think Dad was about six years old—that's what Grandma said. Grandma and Dad opened the crate, dug everything out, and there was a layer of eggs on the bottom. The smell was awful, just horrendous. The vendor had forgotten to take them out. Grandpa laughed so hard remembering that. He was just worried about the pig, didn't give a damn about being careful with those eggs. But there they were, none the worse for wear. Grandma couldn't believe the weight of the piggy bank hadn't crushed those eggs."

Mr. Givand looked at his wife, and the little boy deep in his eyes suddenly brightened. "Maybe you're right. Maybe they're safer in there?"

"John, come on. You were right. I have to have

my rings." She paused, looking down into the sink mournfully. "I never should have taken them off."

She started to cry. "Remember right before your grandpa died? We went to see him in that little dingy apartment. I hated seeing him in that assisted living place. I wish I hadn't looked at the corner of the room where the wallpaper was peeling away because of that leaky ceiling. God, he was so ashamed. You could just see it, the mortification.

"Because he didn't look at me at all, not directly. He didn't fight me with some flip comment the way he used to do. Nothing sarcastic, nothing jovial. No crack with a glint in his eye the way he used to be. Nothing self-piteous, even. He just walked over to his closet and pulled out a tie. Remember? He stood in front of his dresser and he tied that tie so carefully. I can still see it, that back part where the stitching was coming loose. I was so embarrassed, could barely breathe. Then he came over and took me by the arm and led me to that shitty little sink. It was as if he were telling me everything was going to be okay—in his own way. I can still feel his hand on my elbow, guiding me, not letting go, and never admitting he needed help with the walk over to the sink. Just that old-fashioned gentleman taking my arm. He was totally senile. But perfect composure. And he smiled; he knew. Knew how pathetic the place was, knew what it all meant, that he wasn't ever leaving, wasn't ever going to have any trip on any ocean liner ever again." She wouldn't be satisfied until he made the admission about how it all had been. "Remember, John? I know you do."

John crossed his arms, cleared his throat, and nodded, refusing to acknowledge the tears in his eyes.

She went on. "He led you over to his dresser and handed you that change and said, 'For the piggy, Johnny.' It was like you were still a little kid. But it was also like he knew you weren't. He was so serious and so kind. It's like that's how he gave us his blessing about being together. He gave you all the coins in that little tray, remember? Every single one. And those are all in there." She cried. "I didn't mean to leave the rings in the bathroom. I thought I'd put them away in the jewelry box."

"Grandpa would understand, sweetheart. It was an accident."

"It was not an accident. Matthew did it on purpose."

"But he doesn't know."

"My hands are so swollen. I didn't want them to cut the rings off if something were to happen and I had to be delivered immediately."

"Stop crying."

Matthew said, "I know!"

John said, "Then why'd you do it!"

"I didn't do it. I wouldn't do that."

Mrs. Givand said, "Don't lie, Matthew." She hugged her husband and held him and would not let go. "I don't ever want you in a room like that with the wallpaper peeling away from the walls. And we've got to get that long-term care insurance for your father so he doesn't end up in a place like the one your grandfather was in. As soon as possible, this week. We have to find the money."

He pulled her arms away from his neck. "Calm down, honey. That's a different issue. Don't conflate this." He pointed to the pig in the sink. "What should we use?"

She let him go, wiping away her tears. But then recanting everything, feeling it all again, she shook her head, and suddenly decisive and officious she said, "Not the hammer."

"The mallet then?"

"Yes. The mallet. Get the goggles, too."

Her husband went out to the garage to find his tools. She looked at the ceramic pig lying on its side in the sink. It would not have been steady except for the cup of the drain on the other side of the towel. She felt its smooth hard curve. Her son came into the room and stood next to her. She lifted him up. His hand went out to the curve the same way hers had. He cocked his head and patted the bank.

He didn't quite know what was wrong, but sensed it was his fault. "I didn't do it."

"It's okay, Matthew." But it wasn't. Some things just weren't.

She let her son back down, and he returned to his observation station.

She told Matthew the story, but she didn't look at him. She looked at the pig and out the window toward the garage, "Before you were even born this was your daddy's piggy bank. Just like you put your money in it. Did you know that?"

Matthew, always the pragmatist, said, "Why isn't it already full then?"

"It's pretty close." She went on. "And when he was little, like you, he would put his money in this bank. And before that, your daddy's daddy put money in it. Isn't that cool? So you, your daddy, and his daddy all have had a good time finding coins in the sofa or on the sidewalk and putting them in the piggy bank."

She laid her hand on the side of the pig as if soothing it in its last hour. It was lovely—old-fashioned and irreplaceable. It was a Delft design with blue swirls in a creamy glaze. Handcrafted and hand-painted and fired at least four times, she guessed from the variety of blues in the design. They had redecorated Matthew's whole nursery in the same colors to match the pig after Mr. Givand's father had brought it to the house, so proud. She remembered her husband so excited by the pig—he had forgotten it, almost. It had spent so many years in a cardboard box in his father's attic. Having it again brought back everything that was good and decent and safe and right in John's childhood. He had been thrilled to pass all that on to his son.

She looked up at the timbers in the ceiling. God, this child just didn't understand his own legacy.

She felt the pig's four feet, especially the one with

the extra drop of blue glaze at the edge and the one that never quite reached the table top. She looked at the curly raised tail highlighted with sky blue glaze. She looked at the eyes, the snout, the sweet knowing smile. She ran her fingers over the pig's back and felt the slot, the smooth edge where for seventy years the coins had slipped inside.

It must be possible to extract the rings, at least one, one would be enough. She rolled the pig upside down and began shaking it vigorously. She put it back down from the weight and rolled it to have access to the slot. She heaved it again, making the coins cascade inside the glazed beast. She leaned against the counter, and looking into the slot, shook it and peered into the darkness. Grabbing a long kitchen knife she flailed at the slot, jabbing the knife around, up and down, through the coins.

Her husband came through the kitchen door and quickly went to her.

"No, honey! That's not the way. I already tried. Come on."

She was livid. "He's sitting here telling me he didn't do it, when I saw it happen! I almost stopped him. I was right in the doorway. I don't know why I didn't just scream at him or slap him. He knew exactly what he was doing. I saw it in his eyes, that contemptible mischief, the ruin of pure selfishness. I should have put the rings in the safety deposit box. I should have—"

Matthew screamed, "Mommy! I didn't do it!"

John Givand turned toward his son with a vicious hostility, "Matthew, you'd better shut your mouth if you know what's good for you." Mr. Givand held his wife and rocked her slowly until she calmed down. She put the knife back in the drawer and held onto him.

"It's okay." John said. "He didn't know. He just thought the rings were worth something and should go in the bank. They are in the bank. Stand back."

She held his arm for a moment and then gave up, backing away as he shrugged her off. Her hand traveled from her husband's arm, to the countertop, to the oven handle, to the back of a chair which had been in her mother's dining room.

John stood at the sink alone with his duty. He pushed the heavy objects off the edges of the towel, wrapped the soft blue cotton all the way around the pig, shrouding it, preventing ceramic from flying everywhere.

Mrs. Givand steadied herself as she moved slowly

to a safe distance across the kitchen. Her hands ran over the exposed brick—outside for so many years, now inside her kitchen. She motioned to her son through the window.

He knew. This was his punishment—he had to be in the room for the execution. He came into the kitchen and Mrs. Givand picked him up and stood him on a chair so he could see. After a weighted moment she stood next to him.

John Givand took the rubber mallet, pulled the goggles over his face and raised his arms high over his head.

Mrs. Givand wrapped her arms around her son's little round belly, steadying herself as much as him. She leaned over his thick curls.

There was one silent moment.

Then the mallet came down hard into the deep sink. One stroke shattered the ceramic pig inside the towel. Nickels, dimes, pennies, Canadian quarters, and little plastic army men hemorrhaged from the thing, flooding over thick ceramic shards. The morning was silent again after the change rushed out. April sunlight bleaching the floor disappeared again behind a cloud.

Then a bird sang outside in an oak tree. The goggles came off. John Givand, with tears in his eyes, heaved a short breath, ran the change through his fingers searching for the rings.

He sifted handful after handful of change. Where were they? Mrs. Givand touched the top of her son's head, pulled her fingers through his curls, then saw her husband's entire body tighten. He wasn't finding the rings. She left her son and went over to the sink as well. Together, husband and wife, they pulled twenty fingers through the coins.

"No. John. They're here. Just keep looking." Mrs. Givand stacked pennies on the kitchen island, ensuring no rings hid in little towers ten coins high. Then, so much like her son who'd been paralyzed on the couch, she couldn't move. Her consciousness consumed her.

John's hands kept moving over everything in the towel. He pulled coin after coin out of the sink, testing each one between two fingers, as though one might suddenly lose its middle and become his quarry. He said, "Damn it!" when a shard pricked his finger, but kept pulling his hands through.

Nothing.

"Oh my God." He could barely hear himself say it.

She held her breath, couldn't look at him, piled more and more pennies on the island. She grabbed scoopfuls of change out of the sink, poured the coins from one hand to the other, looking, sorting, making sure.

John looked back at her, saw the stacks she was making, immediately began making stacks himself, on the drain board, on the window sill, by the coffee maker, and in front of the container for pasta. "They're not here."

"Keep looking."

She went back to the sink, turned all of the shards over, put them in a pile, got a paper bag, and put the broken ceramic inside. She kept looking for the rings, avoiding the white splinters of pottery lodged in the navy towel. *Where were they?* She picked up the towel, shook it over the island, turned it over to see if the rings could be hanging on the back of it, in some impossibility.

They weren't.

She picked each of the tiny sharp splinters out of the dark cotton, then folded the towel and clung to it, hugged it, wished for it to yield some answer.

It did not.

For a moment between gusts, the only sound in the house was of the upstairs doorknob clicking against the wall in the slight breeze.

She dropped the towel onto the island near the mail.

"I'm telling you. They're not here."

It was too much. She said, "They have to be. I saw him do it."

"What exactly did you see?"

"Don't take that tone with me." It couldn't be her fault. It was her son's fault. It was not her fault.

She saw it happen, watched him do it. "Matthew!"

Her husband didn't care. "I'm asking you a question. What exactly happened?"

"I saw it. I watched him. I couldn't grab them away from him."

"Couldn't grab what away? What did you see?"

"Stop it, John. I told you. I saw him put my wedding rings in your father's stupid piggy bank!"

"Stupid? Now it's stupid?"

"I told you I didn't do it." Matthew ran upstairs and threw himself on his bed.

Wind rushed through the Givands' whole yard. Sunlight flooded back into the kitchen and then as quickly as before, disappeared. Trees swayed and creaked against each other in the bright blue, then gray, then white sky. Through the open doors at the top of the stairs another big gust whooshed in, slid down the staircase, whipped around into the downstairs hallway and it seemed to Mrs. Givand that it hit her right in the face.

"Oh God." She lowered herself into a chair, leaned her elbows on the table, breathed into her clasped hands, and yielded to the new baby's wild endless kicks.

She said to her husband, "He did."

John Givand looked at her but not for long. "Well, they're not in here." John walked through the kitchen's side door and sat down outside on the old concrete step.

She did not go to him, or to her son.

After about twenty minutes, the side door opened again and John came back inside. She did not look up. There was no way she could deal with whatever he was going to say.

But he knew her, said nothing.

She didn't open her eyes, only reached out, put

her hand on his thigh as he stood next to her.

He leaned over and set their son's toy truck down on her placemat.

It was the truck that had been out on the lawn, upsetting him.

She still said nothing, still did not look up. Her other hand went out to the truck and she opened its little toy door, closed it back. John ran one finger down her spine. Her hand moved around his thigh but he shook it off and left her, taking the stairs two at a time to get up to Matthew.

She heard his footsteps slow on the old floorboards of the upstairs hall, heard his gentle two-knuckle knock on the child's bedroom door, heard John go into their son's room right above her, heard the reassuring interplay of their muffled voices, knew the familiar weight of both their bodies moving around to get just perfectly comfortable together on that bright red bed.

She sat up, rolled the faded plastic truck back and forth in front of her, from the knife to the napkin.

HARBINGER OF SPRING

Mr. Lantree still read the newspaper in the kitchen after his lakefront runs. The routine for their days was something they clung to even since he had left his job, which had been around the time they filed the missing person's report, before the Department of Family and Support Services contacted them about their little granddaughter Resa. She'd been found wandering through a SWAT team raid of a boarded-up pillared mansion in Englewood, a southside hell the Lantrees long assumed to be inaccessible.

It wasn't. 63rd & Ashland was just a stop like any other on the circulatory CTA, like theirs even. How many times had Mrs. Lantree walked to Dempster and climbed those iron-capped stairs? Countless.

The couple hadn't even known they had a granddaughter. Someone at the scene that day got a felony charge reduced by disclosing the diapered child's mother's name, though the woman herself had never been accounted for.

So there she was, this little two-year-old, bouncing on her grandpa's knee. Mrs. Lantree, unable to give up, kept going into the city. She was not yet sixty-two and a half.

"I'm late as it is," she said but remained seated next to her husband on one of the kitchen stools that was definitely too tall. She pressed her fingertip against the dark polished rock, picking up a grain or two of spilled salt. Touched her fingertip to her tongue.

Mrs. Lantree missed the melamine counter where she'd stirred sugar cookie dough with her daughter, where they had so carefully pressed bright silver candy balls into cherry-flavored icing. No one had orange kitchens anymore though. So she'd allowed herself to be talked into the black-and-green granite with ancient flecks of mica. She hated it, wanted her old kitchen back, but she said nothing about it, ever. The contractor was a friend's son, building his business, needing the work. He had removed the Pennsylvania Dutch style breakfast nook and put a wide piece of granite in the bay window. Instead of two benches facing each other across the sturdy nicked table, now four stools were all in a row looking out over the front lawn. They had received quite a few compliments on this renovation, but Mrs. Lantree was disgusted by it.

Resa tilted her head from side to side under Mr. Lantree's stubbled chin. It was impossible to know whether he had an impulse to bolt. He might have. People do.

But there was no escape. Mrs. Lantree brushed the other few stray grains of salt onto the floor. "Remember all those silver dragees rolling around everywhere? Oh my God, I thought we'd never clean them up. Like ball bearings, they were. Or buckshot, really. I was so anxious that you might slip and fall. Or, God, that she would." They never said *heroin*—not once, not ever. They looked out the small panes of their big bowed window. All over the lawn, blades of bright green grass were garnering their strength. Black and wet broken-down mulch huddled around the base of twin well-groomed shag-bark hickory trees. After a long winter, one robin stood listening. Mrs. Lantree said, "How does it go?"

"How does what go?" He soothed their fourteen-month-old granddaughter, who was starting to squirm. She tugged at her bib. He unsnapped it, careful not to pinch the skin of her little neck, handed the dirty bib to his wife, bounced the baby girl absently on his lap.

The old habitual patterns were back, so long forgotten. Ee-i-ee-i-oh.

They'd have to do it all all over again—the potty training, the alphabet, telling time. Mrs. Lantree did not say, "Dammit all to hell." She folded the dirty bib, waited for her voice to be steady enough to say, "The spring. Is it trillium, then May apple, then Mertensia?"

"I don't know."

She shoved the dirty bib inside a nearby drawer meant for trivets.

He watched her, said nothing, would very likely take the bib up to the hamper after she left. That's what he likely hated—having to stay, and let go.

She saw his eyes resting on the drawer handle, hurried to get up and away from him. "Yes you do. In the woods. On those dog walks. You know exactly how it goes." She came back to him, darting down upon the table to clear his dishes away. "You just won't tell me. Never tell me anything." Already across the room, she wrapped an apron around her waist, letting the neck ties and chest plate fall away useless.

He watched the robin hopping in the yard.

She faced west toward the street. The water started to get hot, helped by her hand swirling the suds. And she was slow again, back on her familiar perch.

This was two weeks after they had been asked to identify their daughter's remains, which had been found thawing in an alley on Chicago's Westside. Mr. Lantree hummed into the head of the little girl on his lap, kissed her crown, and gave in. "Fine, you're right. It's trillium, May apples, Mertensia, but you forgot harbinger of spring. It comes first. Absolutely first. Before you ever wanted to go walk in the woods with us."

The detective who called had been too young to be tasked with informing anyone's parents of anything. Eagerly, he shared every gory detail. Like a child home from school with a blue ribbon from the science fair, he offered the results of the toxicology report, the likelihood of murder, of prostitution, explained how she was found by an exterminator who'd been spraying for rats, elaborated upon the assumed length of time she'd been left alone out there, frozen, covered in snow, folded into a grocery cart with both legs broken.

Mrs. Lantree coughed her recollection away. Swift again, her heels, gavels each, came down upon the floor.

Both Mr. Lantree and Resa sat frozen until those footsteps stopped.

Perhaps sensing the tensed stillness of her loved ones on heightened alert, Mrs. Lantree dragged a breakfast bar stool a few inches across the floor and sat back down near them both. Resa slipped off her grandpa's lap and ran over to the empty ceramic cat dish. Mr. Lantree had not been ready to release her little round belly.

He watched the child with a longing she did not see. But his wife saw everything and looked away.

They had to find a new proximity, having no way to remain as close as they'd once been.

Mrs. Lantree shifted in her seat. "I never had the right boots for those walks."

Mr. Lantree's irritability flared, just about justified, He directed it toward his wife. "It was her favorite flower."

"You don't know that. She never said anything like that. You're filling in blanks."

"You have no idea what we discussed on those walks. You weren't there."

"The dogs didn't like that slush and mud on the walking trails."

"It wasn't the dogs. It was you not wanting to give the dogs baths and have them get the car muddy."

"Why didn't she tell you she was pregnant? She would have been four months pregnant when you saw her at Eulie's for that last weekly piece of pie."

He did not say that they had had a fight or that they had not had a fight. He did not say whether she had asked for money, or shelter, or medical care. He simply would not tell his wife anything about what had really happened. He only said, "I would have gotten you better boots."

"You never listen."

"*I* never listen? I know she told you. I absolutely know it." What shame was it to either of them to need some kind of new territory for their togetherness of lone lives?

"We had a piece of pie, Maureen. French silk pie. The crust was too cold and soggy underneath. The whipped cream along the edge was dried out, must have been sitting out overnight. That's what we talked about."

"You're lying. You were the last person to see her alive."

"No. The last person to see her alive killed her, Maureen."

Resa ran back to him, crawled up onto his lap, threw her arms around his neck, and buried her face in his shoulder, tired, mad about the raised voices, ready for her morning nap.

Mrs. Lantree reached out toward the child as if to touch her and then recoiled, did not. Instead, she rushed back to her woven area rug, hung a linen calendar towel on the oven handle, took off her apron, went back to the little drawer, took out the bib, and with the speed of a plunging falcon in its hunting stoop she shoved the milk-damp thing deep into her purse. "I never had the right boots."

"It was her favorite flower."

"Their feet would've frozen."

"So what? Dogs don't care. They love it. Every single year you missed harbinger of spring. You missed seeing it with her. You missed her discovering it new again, showing it to you."

She soared away on an updraft of mourning, gasped, held it in, would not release her tears there, not for him to comfort, not for the little girl to see. She was still a stranger, this child. Mrs. Lantree fixed her forward-facing eyes on her husband and said, "I told you, I'm late as it is."

"And I told you I would have gotten you better boots."

The side door slammed.

He heard the old wooden garage door's sections ascend one by one. Heard the old Volvo wagon start up, reliably, while he bounced the weight of his curly-haired granddaughter on his knee.

The robin was gone.

The overgrown baby hung on tightly, wasn't
going anywhere.

Her little body got heavier and heavier with the
coming on of deep sleep, the little breaths came, the small
chest rising and falling against his own, and the hot
sweaty little neck folded itself under his. He rocked,
slowly, imperceptibly. And then, once she was really out,
he just sat, holding her with one arm.

With the other hand he refolded the newspaper,
would have thrown it directly into the recycling bin but
the thing was beyond where he could assure the paper's
successful deposit. Outside he heard the sputtering
screech of a falcon, which had likely driven off the robin.
He slammed his morning news against the counter one
time. But there was no satisfactory snap against the cool,
polished rock which curved where that old orange
melamine had had a real edge. Resa moved a bit in his
arms, but remained asleep.

The paper full of so much that had happened just
lay there.

He forgave the robin for another of its successful
departures and gave up hating the car that took his wife
away, too. It was no one's fault, this moment. Mr. Lantree

cupped the child's head, kissed her crown, and waited—
but couldn't really. He wanted to be rid of it all right then,
wanted only the coming moment when his granddaughter
would wake up, slide down his leg on her own. God he
wanted it to be time for her to be alive enough, free
enough, wise enough, willing enough to just run away,
elated.

ABOUT THE ON IMPULSE SERIES

In an exploration of narrative from catharsis to craft, Nath Jones's writing style develops from the raw, associative, tyrannic rambles of her me-now-more cathartic non-fiction in *The War is Language*, through the delightful rough-hewn vignettes of *2000 Deciduous Trees*, the simple story structures of *Love & Darts*, and finally into *Acquainted with Squalor's* well-rendered literary fiction.

ABOUT THE AUTHOR

Best New American Voices nominee Nath Jones received
an MFA in creative writing from Northwestern
University. Her publishing credits include PANK
Magazine, *There Are No Rules*, and *Sailing World*. She lives
and writes in Chicago.